DEATH
OF A HORSE THIEF

Dolph Scarborough swept the duster aside. A worn Colt .45 rested in a well-oiled holster on his hip. "What the hell are you tryin' to say, mister?"

Luther stepped away from the bar, his right hand dropping casually so that his wrist brushed the grips of the Single Action Army Colt .45 slung low on his hip. His eyes narrowed to slits as he stared into the big man's face. "I'm saying that's my horse."

"You calling me a horse thief?"

Luther shrugged. "Not necessarily. I didn't see who took it. Maybe it was you, maybe not. It doesn't matter. She's still my horse."

Scarborough's knees bent into a crouch, his thick fingers wrapped around the grips of the Colt. Raw rage deepened the flush of the ruddy face. "Damn you! Nobody calls Dolph Scarborough a horse thief!" Scarborough yanked at the pistol.

Scarborough was fast, but not as fast as he thought . . .

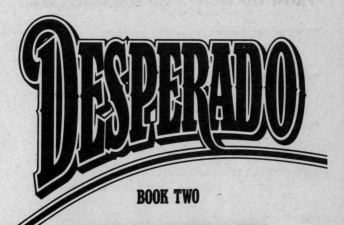

DESPERADO

BOOK TWO

EDGE OF THE LAW
B.W. LAWTON

J

JOVE BOOKS, NEW YORK

DESPERADO #2: EDGE OF THE LAW

A Jove Book / published by arrangement with
the author

PRINTING HISTORY
Jove edition / July 1993

ISBN: 0-515-11133-3

Jove Books are published by The Berkley Publishing Group,
200 Madison Avenue, New York, New York 10016.
The name "JOVE" and the "J" logo
are trademarks belonging to Jove Publications, Inc.

PRINTED IN THE UNITED STATES OF AMERICA

10 9 8 7 6 5 4 3 2 1

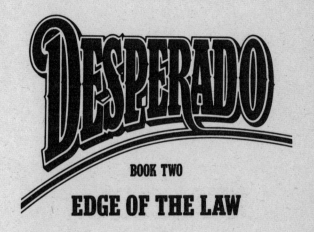

DESPERADO

BOOK TWO

EDGE OF THE LAW

CHAPTER ONE

The rangy brown gelding between Luther McCall's knees sensed trouble a full minute before its rider did.

It showed in the quick flutter of nostrils as the horse snorted nervously and in the alert ears cocked toward the southwest. Luther felt the ripple of anticipation in the horse's wiry but powerful muscles.

Luther knew better than to ignore the signs. When it came to spotting danger, the brown gelding was a better watchdog than any hound. A man who paid no attention to what his horse was trying to tell him didn't last long in this part of the West.

After a moment, Luther dropped a hand to the horse's withers, a signal of reassurance. "Easy, Chili," he said softly, "I see it now." Luther's hand dropped to the stock of the Winchester rifle in its saddle scabbard as he squinted toward the faint smudge of smoke, flattened into a soft gray mist by the southwest wind. The smoke sifted from the mouth of a shallow valley beyond a rocky ridge in the broken hills north of the Cimarron River.

Smoke could mean several things, all of them trouble. Especially here in the place called the Cimarron Strip, a no-man's-land populated by outlaws, an occasional band of bronco Indians who had bolted the reservation, or the nervous trigger fingers of wanderers who drifted into this stretch of wild country.

The tracks of the six men and the remuda of twenty stolen horses Luther followed were fresh, less than a day old. And the trail led straight toward the smoke. Luther damn well intended to catch up with the band, but on his own terms.

That didn't include riding into the middle of a half dozen gunmen in broad daylight.

Luther couldn't have cared less about nineteen of the stolen horses; they belonged to a rich rancher back in Kansas, a man who built his fortune on other people's sweat. But the men up ahead had made one mistake.

One of the horses they had stolen belonged to Luther McCall.

Luther slipped the Winchester Model 73 from its scabbard, cracked the lever to make sure a cartridge was chambered and ready, then reined Chili toward a cluster of stunted junipers at the crest of the ridge. He pulled the brown to a stop just below the crest, swung down, and made his way to the top. The wind-twisted evergreens gave him a good vantage point to check out the valley unobserved. He slid between two junipers, the oily scent of the trees heavy in his nostrils, and stared toward the valley below.

The remains of a settler's cabin lay a hundred yards away. Embers still winked in the charred logs. A slight shift of the wind brought a belly-wrenching scent to Luther's nostrils—the smell of burned human flesh. He pulled the Winchester hammer to full cock. There was no sign of movement, no hint of life in the valley below.

Behind the smoldering logs that had been the cabin was a wrecked corral and a half dugout that must have been used as a storage room or small barn. A jumbled woodpile lay halfway between the house and downed corral poles. A shallow, spring-fed creek bristling with wild berry vines twisted its way around the corral, flowed past the remnants of the cabin, and finally disappeared into a boggy seep beyond an overturned outhouse to the south. A pair of buzzards circled overhead. Luther doubted there would be much left for the scavengers after the fire died down.

He watched and waited for almost a half hour, saw nothing, and finally worked his way back down the ridge to his horse. "Damn fool nesters probably deserved whatever they got," Luther grumbled aloud. "No man with a lick of sense would settle in a godforsaken place like this." He stepped into the saddle, sheathed the Winchester, and kneed Chili into motion. He was about to circle the homestead and pick up the horse thieves' tracks on the other side when he decided to give the place a closer check. Those buzzards up there might know something I don't, he thought.

The stench of burned flesh was almost overpowering in what would have been the front yard of the cabin. Luther's nose wrinkled in revulsion at the scent. Chili didn't like it either. The brown snorted and danced sideways, skittish, as Luther urged the horse closer to the ruins. Luther didn't bother to dismount. There was nothing to see afoot that he couldn't see from horseback. Two charred, grotesquely twisted bodies lay in one corner of the cabin. If the dead settlers had possessed anything of value, it was long gone now, lining the pockets of a half dozen horse thieves.

"Hold it right there, mister!"

Luther's right hand slapped against the butt of the Colt hung low on his right hip at the unexpected sound. But something about the challenge stayed his hand; he didn't draw the weapon. The voice was thin, weak, and high-pitched. The call came from the edge of the tangle of berry vines along the creek.

Luther turned toward the thicket and felt his eyebrows lift in surprise. A sandy-haired boy who couldn't have been more than a dozen years old knelt at the edge of the thicket, his clothes smudged and torn. Blood soaked the left shoulder of a tattered shirt. He held a rifle, the small black hole in the muzzle wavering slightly but not straying far from Luther's chest. A .22 caliber bullet was bad news, Luther knew. Not because of its power, but because it made a dirty little hole. More men had died from infection caused by puny .22 slugs than from the heavy wallop of a .45.

"Son," Luther said casually, "you can get yourself dead pointing a gun at a man."

"And you can get just as dead if I pull this trigger." The boy's voice quavered, but the tone was serious. "You men took everything we had. Ain't nothing left to take. What did you come back for?"

"I had nothing to do with this. Just passing through and saw the smoke."

The boy squinted down the rifle barrel as if he were struggling to focus his eyes on the big man on the brown horse. The youth's face was almost stark white beneath the dirt and grime.

"I'll shoot if you move," the boy said. Under the weak and shaky words was a distinct note of determination. The kid's got sand, Luther thought. He slowly raised his hand from the butt of the colt.

"What happened here, boy?"

"Some men came. They killed my pa and my uncle. Shot me before I could use this rifle. I reckon they thought I was dead, too." The voice was rapidly growing weaker. "They burnt the house and stole our stock."

"Was one of the men big, like me? Wearing a duster and riding a black mare with a white star on her face?"

The rifle muzzle steadied on Luther's chest. "You know 'em, then?"

"Son, I've been tracking those horse thieves all the way from Kansas."

"You a lawman?"

Luther shook his head. "No. I'm just a man who wants to get his horse back." He stared toward the boy's bloody shirt. "Looks like you got hit pretty hard. You plan to stand there and bleed to death, or are you going to put that rifle down and let me help you?"

Indecision flickered in the boy's eyes. "How do I know you won't kill me?"

"You don't," Luther said, "and I like a man smart enough not to trust a stranger. For what it's worth, you have my word on it."

The youth's eyelids drooped. Luther could tell the lad was staying awake only by strength of will, and the boy had more of that than most grown men. After a moment the rifle muzzle wavered, then dropped.

"All right, mister. I reckon I'm likely to die anyway."

"Everyone does, eventually." Luther swung from the saddle and strode toward the boy, keeping most of his attention on the little .22 rifle bore. Luther McCall never took anything for granted. It was a good way to get dead. "The trick, son, is to put off that time as long as possible." He reached out, lifted the scarred Remington rolling-block single-shot rifle from the youth's hand, and put the weapon carefully on the ground. "Now, let's take a look at that bullet hole." He pulled the bloody remnants of the boy's shirt back.

It was a nasty wound. A large caliber bullet had hit the youth at an angle in the upper back, deflected off the shoulder blade, and tore away a sizeable chunk of muscle when it came out at the top of his shoulder. The kid had to be hurting something fierce, Luther knew, but his eyes were still dry and the small, square jaw was set in defiance of the pain. Luther was reasonably sure the slug hadn't cut any major blood vessels, or the boy would have been dead by now. But he had lost a hell of a lot of blood from a small frame.

"How—how bad is it?"

Luther sighed and shook his head. "Bad enough to worry about. We have to get that bleeding stopped right away." He stepped away for a moment, rummaged in a saddlebag, pulled out his one remaining clean shirt and a bottle of clear liquid. He lifted his canteen and returned to the youth's side. "This is going to hurt like old billy hell, son," Luther said, "but it's got to be done."

The boy ground his teeth against a fresh wave of pain, then nodded. "Couldn't hurt a lot more than it does now. Let's get it done."

Luther heard the air whistle through the boy's nostrils in a silent cry of agony as Luther dabbed the gore away from bullet-ravaged muscle. The boy didn't scream or even groan aloud. Tough little guy, Luther thought; most grown men would be whimpering like babies by now.

His admiration for the sandy-haired boy's courage grew as he worked on the wound. "You have a name, son?"

"Jimmy—Jimmy Macko." The words were slurred through clenched teeth.

"Well, Jimmy Macko, you're *hombre mucho*," Luther said. He finished cleaning the wound. The shoulder blade was probably cracked, if not broken, by the impact of the bullet, but the shoulder joint was intact. Luther struggled in sweaty silence for several minutes, dribbling raw alcohol onto torn flesh and swabbing it down. He heard the grind of small teeth against the blast of fiery pain from the disinfectant. Still, the boy remained conscious. No tears streaked the dirty face.

Luther opened a small leather pouch at his belt, dribbled a mixture of herb leaves and ground tobacco onto the wound until the bleeding eased, then tore his clean shirt into sections. He bandaged the wound as best he could and tied the pad into place with strips ripped from the shirtsleeves. Finally, he stepped back and swiped a hand over his own sweaty forehead.

"That's about the best I can do for you out here, son," Luther said. "You need a doctor. Is there one around here?"

"Cim—Cimarron." The boy's voice was barely audible now, muted by pain, shock, and loss of blood. He nodded toward the south. "Ain't much . . . of a town. No real doctor. But the marshal's wife's . . . nursed a lot of hurts."

Luther winced inwardly at the mention of the word *marshal*. He had no use for lawmen and good reasons for staying clear of them. He also found himself resenting the time he would lose in taking the boy into town. That would let the horse thieves gain a few more hours on him. But he wasn't worried about losing the trail. Six men and twenty horses left a wide track, and by now he had a pretty good idea where they were headed.

What bothered Luther most was that he had been dealt a hand in a game he hadn't intended to play. The business on the homestead wasn't his affair. If the boy had been a man grown, Luther would have had no qualms about mounting the brown and riding off to leave the wounded one to his own fate. But a kid—especially this particular kid—was a horse of a different breed. Luther McCall would never admit it, but he almost liked kids. If circumstances had been different, if he hadn't had a price on his head and every bounty hunter, lawman, and would-be gunslinger in the West after his hair, he would have liked to have kids of his own. A man should leave something of himself behind when the sun went down for the last time.

He glanced at the boy. Jimmy's head nodded, the eyelids almost closed. He was fighting it hard, but he was on the thin edge of unconsciousness. One thing was for sure: Jimmy Macko, all twelve years' worth, was a scrapper.

Luther saw something of himself in the sandy-haired boy, a toughness that wouldn't let him cry from pain or loss.

"Mister?"

"Yes, Jimmy?"

"Pa—and Uncle Ed—"

"There's nothing we can do for them. They're gone. Maybe you can ask the marshal of this town to send somebody out to bury the—to bury them." Luther sighed. "We can't spare the time, son. We've got to get you some real help."

Luther gathered up the reins and led the snorting brown to the boy's side. "We'll have to ride double," he said, "and I'm not sure old Chili here is going to like that. He's twitchy at times."

"Chili . . . funny name . . . for a horse."

Luther almost smiled. "It fits. He's full of pepper and gives me a bellyache most of the time." Luther studied the brown and his rig. There wouldn't be much room for two riders, even if one of them wasn't a lot bigger than a mite. The single-fire saddle already carried two rifles—a Sharps Fifty for long-range work and the Winchester for closer action—a bedroll, a possibles sack that held a few cooking utensils and a handful of food, and two saddlebags. The brown's eyes were wide, the whites showing all around, and the nostrils flared at the smell of blood.

Luther tied his canteen back onto the saddle and knelt beside the boy. "Might as well give it a try, Jimmy," he said. "Let's see how Chili feels about it."

He helped the boy to his feet and, talking softly to the snorting, walleyed brown, eased Jimmy into the saddle. Chili shied a bit, stomped his feet and tossed his head, then settled down under Luther's firm hand. Luther toed the stirrup.

"Mister?" Jimmy's voice was strained and growing fainter under the renewed agony of movement in mounting the horse.

"Yes?"

"My . . . rifle. Don't forget . . . rifle."

Luther stooped, retrieved the little Remington, checked the action—there was a live round in the chamber—and lowered the hammer. "What do you need it for?"

"To . . . to kill those . . . men someday. For what they . . . what they did here."

Luther slipped the short rifle beneath the straps of his bedroll. "Can't think of a better reason to keep it around, Jimmy," he said. "Now, let's get into town. Before you pass out on me, tell me which way to ride."

The boy described a few prominent landmarks as Luther mounted and settled himself in the saddle, careful not to jostle Jimmy more than necessary. He reined the antsy brown toward the south. "Let's go find Cimarron."

The town was little more than a handful of adobe shacks, picket corrals, and a couple of log homes nestled beside a grove of cottonwoods and wispy willows in a bend of the river. A well with walls of reddish-brown native sandstone stood in the center of what would have been the town square if Cimarron had grown to its founders' expectations. At the east end of the street stood the only clapboard structure in the settlement, a whitewashed building topped with a steeple and bell tower. The church dominated the approach to Cimarron, the white boards and splashes of color from flower beds lending the only break to an otherwise adobe-and-sand tinted landscape. An ancient cannon that looked like a leftover from the Mexican War stood in a circle of stones a few feet from the church.

Luther eased the brown to a stop and studied the town with care, a habit he had developed over years of riding through the West. A cautious man made sure he knew the lay of the land before heading into unfamiliar territory. The main street was all but deserted. A single spring wagon stood beside an abandoned harness shop. Two horses waited half asleep outside a low building that seemed to be Cimarron's only saloon. Luther saw nothing that seemed to pose an immediate threat. The raiders wouldn't likely be here. Luther would have crossed their tracks if they had turned in this direction, and a herd of twenty horses would stand out like a clipper ship under full sail in the middle of a nowhere like this. He touched heels to Chili. The brown stepped out gingerly toward the settlement of Cimarron.

Jimmy's head lay back against Luther's shoulder as the two rode down the wide, dusty path that served as Cimarron's only through street. The pain, exhaustion, and emotional toll of the past hours had finally dulled Jimmy's stubborn will. Luther knew the boy was better off for being unconscious.

He kept his left arm around the boy's waist to hold him in the saddle, the reins gripped loosely in his big left fist. He kept his right hand close to the holstered Colt as they passed a vacant adobe at the edge of town.

A tall, thin man with a potbelly that seemed out of place on such a skinny frame leaned against the doorway of one nearby building, a broom in his hand. A faded, hand-lettered sign marked the building as Holloway's Emporium and General Store. The thin man stiffened as he stared toward the approaching riders.

Luther reined Chili to a stop a dozen feet from the thin man. "Looking for the marshal," Luther said. "I've got a boy here who's been hurt pretty bad."

The shopkeeper's brown eyes squinted suspiciously. "You the one hurt him?"

Luther leveled a hard gaze at the shopkeeper's face. His eyes were cold and hard as he fought to control the sudden flare of temper in his gut. "I said I'm looking for the marshal."

The merchant tried to hold Luther's stare and failed. He turned and pointed a long, thin finger toward a small adobe building at the end of the street next to the church. "Marshal's office is down there. Last building on the left. He won't be there now."

"Then where the hell is he?" Luther heard the icy tone in his own voice. "I don't intend to stand here and play word games with you, dammit."

The storekeeper shrugged. "He'd be at his house this time of day. The one next to the office."

Luther didn't reply. He kneed Chili into motion, then pulled the brown to a stop outside the adobe. "Hello, the house!" he called.

A moment later the door swung open. A weathered, aging man with skin the color of well-tanned leather limped onto the narrow porch. He leaned heavily on a cane. Luther saw at a glance that the man's left leg had been mangled. The old man's thick hair and drooping handlebar mustache were almost pure white, a stark contrast to the brown skin and deep hazel eyes. He carried no weapon. Alarm glittered in the old man's eyes as he stared at the boy in the saddle.

"Are you the marshal?" Luther asked.

The old man nodded. "What did you to do Jimmy?"

"I didn't do anything except patch him up a bit. He's been shot. Hurt pretty bad. Before he passed out he asked me to bring him here."

The marshal twisted his head toward the open doorway and shouted, "Martha, get out here! Jimmy's hurt!" He limped from the porch, his cane thumping the dust with each stride. He moved pretty well for a lame man. Luther heard quick footsteps on the flooring inside the house, then a woman stepped through the doorway. She was stocky, heavy in the hips and shoulders. Tendrils of brown hair laced with gray stuck to her forehead in the heat. She glanced at Luther, a quick stab of expressive green eyes, then at the boy.

"Oh, dear God," she said. Luther heard the genuine worry in her voice. "What happened?"

"He's been shot, Martha. He doesn't look too good," the marshal answered.

Martha was at Luther's stirrup in seconds, her hands held out. She glanced at the marshal. "Don't just stand there, Josh Turlock," she snapped at the man with the cane. "We've got to get this boy inside, quick."

Luther eased the unconscious Jimmy into waiting hands, then dismounted and followed as Turlock and his wife carried the youth inside. Martha led the way to a small back room where a single cot waited beneath a window. It was mercifully cool inside the thick adobe walls. They placed the boy facedown on the cot. Martha turned his head so that he could breathe, adjusted a pillow beneath his cheek, and brushed a sweaty cowlick from the boy's forehead with a gentle hand.

"What happened to him?" Martha asked as she pulled aside the bloody bandage that had been Luther's clean shirt.

"Some hard cases raided his place," Luther said. "They shot Jimmy, and killed his father and uncle." He heard Martha's low clucking sound as she peeled away the makeshift bandage and glanced at the wound. The marshal leaned forward to peer over her shoulder.

"Lord, the poor child . . ." The woman's voice trailed away, choked with tears of hurt and sympathy.

"He's more than a child, ma'am," Luther said solemnly. "That youngster is a man in a kid's body. He's a tough little nut. Never cried, not once."

Luther became aware that the marshal had turned away from the cot and was studying Luther through narrowed lids. Suspicion and growing anger smoldered in the hazel eyes.

"Mister," the marshal said, "I think you and me better have a little talk."

"Do your talking in the living room, Josh," Martha said. "I'll call for help if I need it." She pushed up the sleeves of her homemade housedress and bent over the small form on the cot.

Marshal Josh Turlock waved toward the door and followed Luther into the combination living and dining room. It was the largest room in the house, the furniture old but sturdy and comfortable. Luther turned to face the marshal. Josh Turlock didn't invite him to sit down.

"All right, mister," the marshal said, "tell me what happened out at Jimmy's place. And it better be a good story, because I'm not real sure about you just yet."

Luther stared straight into the lawman's eyes. The gleam of suspicion was still there. Josh Turlock was not carrying a weapon and Luther was, but if the marshal was worried about that little item it didn't show in the cold hazel eyes. Luther recounted the events of the day. Turlock listened without outward expression, then finally nodded as Luther finished his account.

"Any idea who did it?"

"Probably that bunch I was tracking," Luther said. He heard the hard edge growing in his own voice. "Six men. Leader goes by the name of Dolph Scarborough."

The marshal's eyebrows bunched. "Heard of Scarborough. Missouri redleg, as I recollect. Bad hombre. Wanted in six, seven states. How well do you know him?"

Luther shrugged. "Well enough to know he stole a good horse from me. And," he added pointedly, "he's gaining ground on me while we're standing here talking."

"Maybe." The marshal's voice went cold and flat. "But I reckon you can spare a few more minutes." He studied Luther's face again. "You look kind of familiar, mister. You got a name?"

"Most people have."

"I don't reckon you'd be interested in sharing that bit of information with an old town marshal?"

Luther felt his eyes narrow into slits, the tension build in his muscles. He didn't like questions from anybody. Especially lawmen.

"Travis," he said.

"First name or last?"

"Just Travis will do."

Josh Turlock glared hard into Luther's eyes for a moment, then unexpectedly chuckled. "I guess it will, at that. Any relation to Colonel William Barrett Travis of the Alamo?"

The tension drained from Luther's body as quickly as it had built. A slight grin tugged at the corners of his mouth. "My sainted pappy, sir," he said. "Got himself killed a few years before I was born."

The marshal chuckled and shook his head. "I figured you might be able to spin a man a yarn." The gleam of amusement faded from the hazel eyes. "But I don't think you're yarning me about what happened out there. Far as I'm concerned, you're free to go." Josh Turlock plucked a battered pipe from a vest pocket and stuffed the bowl. He cocked an eyebrow at Luther as he struck a match. "Travis, if you're planning to go after Scarborough, you might consider taking some help along. There's more than one Scarborough. Dolph's brother Tyler is the meaner of the two. And he's got a bunch of hired guns around him most of the time."

Luther shook his head. "I work alone, Marshal."

Turlock fired the pipe and squinted through the smoke. "Watch your back, Travis, and good luck."

Luther nodded and turned toward the door.

"Travis," the marshal said, his voice soft, "thanks for bringing Jimmy in alive. That boy's like the son Martha and I never had. We've known him since he was no bigger than a hound dog pup. We're obliged."

Luther raised fingertips to his hat brim in salute. "Just take care of him, Marshal. I've seen enough gunshot wounds to know he's not out of the woods yet."

"Like you said, he's tough. And he's in good hands. Martha's better with sick or hurt folks than any doctor in two hundred miles of here." The marshal dragged at the pipe and followed Luther out the door.

Luther mounted and started to rein away, then hesitated. "Almost forgot. Jimmy wanted this." He slid the little .22 single-shot rifle from his bedroll and handed it to the marshal. Then he kneed Chili toward the west down the main street of Cimarron.

At the edge of town, Luther twisted in the saddle to glance back down the street. Marshal Josh Turlock still stood on the porch, leaning against his cane and working the pipe as he stared in Luther's direction. Probably still trying to get a handle on me, Luther thought. He hoped the old coot didn't remember every wanted flier that came across his desk.

He pushed the thought aside. There was some unfinished business up ahead. La Cueva was less than three days' ride. And if Luther knew outlaws and horse thieves, that's where he would find Dolph Scarborough's bunch. With any luck at all, he'd find them before they could sell the big black.

CHAPTER
TWO

Luther McCall lounged against the stained pine bar of the La Cueva Cantina and sipped at a mug of lukewarm beer, waiting and watching.

Trail grime stained his clothes and his disposition in equal amounts. The ride across northern New Mexico from Raton Pass in the northeast to this little town in the rugged Sangre de Cristo Mountains had taxed even the leggy brown's endurance. It had been a tough ride over country broken by deep river gorges and steep, twisting mountain trails, 80 miles in a straight line but closer to 120 on horseback. Still, he hadn't been all that far behind the outlaws with the stolen horses. Maybe they hadn't had time to sell the black yet.

Luther let his gaze sweep the saloon once more and was satisfied that none of the men he stalked were among the scant crowd of early afternoon drinkers.

At a table a few feet to Luther's left, three young men played a listless game of penny-ante poker. Out of work cowboys looking for a brand to ride for, Luther figured. Most of the ranch jobs in northern New Mexico and western Texas were already taken. And with a drought building, there would be few chances for even a top hand to land more than a month's work at a time during roundup.

A grizzled old-timer with the look of a prospector about him hunched over a table near the door, a whiskey glass in his hand. Probably still dreaming about that one big strike, Luther thought. The only other drinkers in the place were a middle-aged man in a silk suit and tie, most likely a buyer of stolen stock, and a tall, gangly shopkeeper or undertaker

14

type. Luther figured the place would liven up considerably along about sundown.

He had chosen his drinking spot with his customary care. From where he stood with his back to the wall, he had a reasonably good view of the street through the open doorway and the smoke-stained plate glass window that faced La Cueva's main thoroughfare. There had been little traffic along the street for the last couple of hours.

Luther tried to control the boredom that was beginning to settle over him. Waiting wasn't his best hole card. But more than once it had paid off. A hunter who let the game come to him stood a better chance of bagging the animal than a man who went charging around the countryside. Sooner or later, some or all of Scarborough's gang would feel the urge for whiskey or women, or both, and La Cueva was the best place to find them for miles around. It was also the best place in New Mexico to dispose of stolen livestock. That seemed to be the town's biggest industry. Luther doubted there was a critter with hide and four hooves within a hundred miles that actually belonged to its rightful owner. The tracks of the stolen horses had led straight to La Cueva before Luther lost the trail in the growing maze of other hoofprints.

Luther glanced up as a new bartender came on duty, taking the soiled apron from the sour-faced man who had grudgingly gotten up from his stool when absolutely necessary to serve the few customers in the place.

The new bartender lumbered toward Luther. The barkeep was as broad as he was tall, most of it in rolls of fat around his jowls and belly.

"Another beer, friend?" The bartender's voice was high and squeaky. It seemed out of place in a man of such bulk.

Luther downed the last swallow of the nearly flat beer, nodded, and handed the mug to the barkeep. The heavy glass thumped back before him a few moments later.

"That'll be a dime, friend."

Luther glanced at the mug. The top third of it was nothing but foam. He lifted a cold gaze to the fat man's eyes. "I think a nickel's more like it," he said flatly.

The bartender's face reddened. "Price is a dime, mister," he said.

"Half the mug, half the price." Luther felt his eyes narrow in growing irritation. He wasn't in the mood to take much crap off anybody today. "I pay for what I'm served. I ordered a beer, not a glass of calf slobbers."

The barkeep's left hand dropped below the level of the bar top. "Listen, fella," he said, "we don't put up with troublemakers and bellyachers in this place."

A muscle in Luther's jaw twitched. "If you touch that gun under there, you won't ever have to listen to anybody complain again." Luther's tone was hard and deadly.

The bartender stared at Luther for a moment as if measuring him. Luther was used to being stared at. A man who stood a touch over six feet tall and carried two hundred pounds of solid muscle along with a big Colt revolver and a heavy bladed Damascus knife got stared at a lot. His pale blue eyes with only a bit more color than ice, thick chestnut mustache and a day's stubble of beard, and flat-crowned, wide-brimmed plainsman style hat that was liberally stained with sweat and travel dirt made a package that naturally drew people's attention.

Luther still didn't care much for being stared at.

Beads of nervous sweat broke out on the fat man's forehead and upper lip. His mouth twitched at the corners. Luther became aware of the almost complete silence that had fallen over the saloon. The low mutters of the card players stopped as the tension grew and spread.

The barkeep made up his mind. He slowly brought his hand above the bar and forced a weak grin. "Ah, what the hell," he said with a shrug. "I reckon you got a gripe comin'. I'll knock some of that head off for you."

He lumbered back a minute later. This time the mug was full, with just enough foam to stir the flavor of hops and malt. Luther fished a dime from his shirt pocket and dropped it on the bar. "Better," he said.

The bartender reached for the dime, then paused and swallowed. He left the coin untouched. "On the house, mister. Call it my mistake." The fat man turned away and waddled over to carry another bottle to the old prospector.

"About damn time somebody called that pork belly's hand," one of the young cowboys said softly. "He's shorted us on drinks every time he's been on duty." The cowhand pushed back his chair and stood. "I'm tapped out, boys. Man knows he's flat busted when he can't even play penny-ante poker any longer." The young man stepped to the bar a few feet from Luther and turned to face him. "Know where a man can get a job here, mister?"

Luther shook his head. "Don't know the country."

"Just passing through?"

Luther felt the aggravation rise again, but held it in check. The cowboy's tone wasn't nosy. He was probably as bored as Luther and just looking for conversation that he hadn't already heard before. Luther sipped at the beer. "Looking for a horse."

The cowboy grinned. "Reckon you've come to the right place. La Cueva's full of 'em. You're not too choosy about where they come from, you'll make out. Any particular type you have in mind?"

Luther glanced out the window and felt his muscles tense. "I just found her," he said softly.

On the street outside, a big man on a star-faced black horse yanked at a rein and rammed a spur into the animal's ribs. A surge of anger shot through Luther's body. He had no use for a man who mistreated a horse. Especially when the animal happened to be his.

"The black? That's Dolph Scarborough's new horse," the cowboy said. "I don't expect she's for sale. . . ." The young man's voice trailed off as he looked closer into Luther's eyes. He turned away, hurried back to the poker table, and eased himself into a chair.

Luther ignored the cowboy and focused his attention on the big man on the black. He watched and waited as Dolph Scarborough dismounted and tied the reins to the hitch rail outside the cantina. The horseman stomped through the door, made his way to the bar, and slammed a ham-sized fist onto the bar top.

"Hey, Jules! Get a bottle over here," Scarborough called to the barkeep. "You got a thirsty customer. And make it the good stuff, not that bellyache sheep-dip you dribble out for bar whiskey."

Luther studied the man as Dolph Scarborough swept the bottle to him, poured a water glass half full of whiskey, and downed the contents in three long swallows. Up close, Scarborough looked even bigger than he had on horseback. Luther figured he stood about six three, with thick, heavy shoulders and forearms beneath the stained linen duster he wore. The broad, stubbled face carried a skewed nose that had obviously been broken; dense, wiry black eyebrows framed surprisingly small and close-set black eyes. The knuckles of the hand that held the glass were a mass of scar tissue. Barroom brawler, Luther thought as he sized up the big man. He wondered if he could take Scarborough in an old-fashioned, knockdown, drag-out fistfight, but quickly dismissed the thought. Luther McCall wasn't in La Cueva for any knuckle skinning.

Luther shifted the beer mug to his left hand and stared at Dolph Scarborough. After a moment the big man seemed to sense Luther's gaze and shifted his bulk to face him.

"What the hell you starin' at, feller?" Scarborough's voice was deep and resonant, the piggish eyes glaring in irritation.

"Just thinking," Luther said, his tone smooth and conversational. He forced a slight smile. "That's a mighty fine-looking horse you're riding."

The challenge in Scarborough's eyes faded slightly. "You got a good eye for horseflesh, mister."

"I know a good mount when I see one." Luther kept his voice calm and level. "I believe I'll take her."

Scarborough grinned. "She ain't for sale."

Luther smiled back. "I didn't say I'd buy her. I said I believe I'll take her. Or you might say take her *back*."

The grin faded from the big man's face. He swept the duster aside. A worn Colt .45 rested in a well-oiled holster on his hip. "What the hell are you tryin' to say, mister?"

Luther stepped away from the bar, his right hand dropping casually so that his wrist brushed the grips of the Single Action Army Colt .45 slung low on his hip. His eyes narrowed to slits as he stared into the big man's face. "I'm saying that's my horse."

Luther heard the sudden scrape and clatter of chairs as the three cowboys at the nearby table scrambled out of the line of fire. Catching a stray slug in a barroom gunfight could spoil a man's day in a hurry.

Dolph Scarborough's broad face flushed beneath the dense stubble. "You calling me a horse thief?"

Luther shrugged. "Not necessarily. I didn't see who took the black. Maybe it was you, maybe not. It doesn't matter. She's still my horse."

Scarborough's knees bent into a crouch, his thick fingers wrapped around the grips of the Colt. Raw rage deepened the flush of the ruddy face. "Damn you! Nobody calls Dolph Scarborough a horse thief!" Scarborough yanked at the pistol.

Scarborough was fast, but not as fast as he thought. The barrel of his Colt hadn't cleared leather before Luther's first slug hammered into the second button of his shirt. The impact of the .45 slug knocked a grunt from the big man. Luther let the recoil of the Peacemaker settle, thumbed the hammer back as the weapon fell into line, and squeezed the trigger. Scarborough stumbled back a step as the soft lead thumped into his gut. Still, he didn't go down; he struggled to lift his Colt with a hand weakened by shock and disbelief. The muzzle wavered, came up a few inches.

Luther took half a heartbeat to steady his aim and fired again. Scarborough's head snapped back as a thumb-sized hole sprouted at the bridge of his nose; the back of his head exploded in a red mist and sent his hat flying. The pistol dropped, spun from limp fingers. Dolph Scarborough was dead before his shoulders hit the floor of the saloon.

Luther squinted through the thick haze of blue-gray powder smoke, saw at an instant that Scarborough would never again be a problem, and spun to face the cowboys standing along the far wall. All three stood with their hands held well away from their weapons. Disbelief widened the eyes of the young man who had spoken to Luther.

"You boys want a hand in this?" Luther said calmly.

All three shook their heads emphatically. "No way, mister," one of them said, his voice shaky. "I ain't catching lead over a private argument."

Luther nodded. He glanced toward the old prospector. The man hadn't moved; he lifted an eyebrow at Luther as if to say "good shooting," and raised his glass in a silent toast. The fat bartender stood beside the prospector's table, eyes wide and face pale in surprise and shock. He wouldn't be a threat.

Luther worked the ejector rod of the Colt, kicked the empties free of the chamber, and casually thumbed fresh loads into the weapon before dropping it back in the holster. He lifted his beer with his left hand, drained the mug, and plopped it back onto the bar. He strode from the saloon into the bright sunlight and reached for the reins of the snorting black mare.

Luther stripped the dead man's saddle and blanket from the black and let the equipment drop into the street. His ears still rang from the concussion of muzzle blasts in the saloon. He heard the rising mutter of voices from within, then the sound of booted feet approaching at a run.

"You there!" The voice came from a wiry man carrying a shotgun. The man skidded to a stop in the street ten paces from Luther. Sunlight glinted from a badge pinned to an expensive leather vest. "Hold it! What the hell's going on here?"

Luther stared hard at the little man with the big shotgun. "Just unsaddling my horse," he said. The blood rage from the gunfight still boiled in Luther's veins. The sight of the star did nothing to calm his mind or ease the ache building in his clenched jaws.

"I heard shots."

"This horse was stolen from me. The man who rode her in didn't want to give her back," Luther said. "Decided to pull a gun on me. He was downright unreasonable about the whole affair. It got him dead."

The man behind the badge glanced quickly toward the saloon, then back at Luther. He cocked one barrel of the double shotgun. "Drop that gun belt, mister."

Luther shook his head. "I don't think so."

The lawman lifted the muzzles of the shotgun. "I said drop it. Nobody's fast enough to pull a handgun before I can squeeze the trigger on this smoothbore."

"Don't count on it, sheriff," a voice from beside the saloon door said. "This man just killed Dolph Scarborough. Dolph had his gun half out before this fellow even moved. And it still wasn't even close."

The sheriff glanced at the speaker. The young cowboy leaned against the saloon door, thumbs hooked in his belt. "It was a fair fight," he said. "I'd say this man gave Dolph more of an edge than anybody deserved."

Surprise widened the lawman's eyes. "You killed Dolph Scarborough?"

Luther shrugged. "He had a choice. He made the wrong one." Luther heard the clatter of boots and shoes as a handful of men began to filter toward the saloon, drawn by the gunfire.

The lawman's eyes narrowed in renewed challenge. "I'm going to take you in, mister. Nobody kills a man in my county and just rides off like nothing happened."

Luther let his right hand brush the familiar leather of the holster. "And nobody takes my gun, sheriff. So it looks like we've got a standoff here. I suppose it's your move now."

A murmur spread through the growing crowd. At the corner of his vision Luther saw the crowd part, drawing well away from the potential showdown in the street. Buckshot or a .45 slug didn't care what or who it hit once a trigger got pulled. Caution and fear moved men a lot quicker than curiosity did. For a few tense heartbeats the sheriff stared into Luther's face. Then the shotgun muzzles wavered under the icy glare from the pale blue eyes. He slowly lowered the weapon. "All right, mister. For now, you keep the hog leg. Just don't go riding off until I find out for sure just what the hell happened here." The lawman nodded toward the cantina. "Let's go take a look. You first."

Luther sighed, retied the black's reins to the hitch rail, and stepped into the adobe building. The sheriff and the young cowboy followed.

The acrid scent of burned black powder and coppery smell of blood lingered amid the stale beer and tobacco odor in the bar. The bartender with the big gut leaned against the bar, his jowly face the color of ashes. Scarborough lay where he had fallen, sightless eyes staring at the ceiling. Blood soaked the dead man's shirtfront and oozed from the dark hole at the bridge of his nose. The old prospector still sat nearby, sipping at a fresh shot of whiskey.

Luther heard the sheriff's sharp intake of breath behind him. The lawman knelt beside the body for a moment, then stood and glanced around.

"Jesse said this man"—the sheriff waved the shotgun muzzle in Luther's direction—"shot Dolph. Anybody else want to talk about it?"

The old prospector grunted. "Dolph had it coming, Bates. He tried to pull iron on this big fellow here. Turns out old Dolph made a mistake. No big loss."

A mutter of agreement rippled through the crowd in the saloon. "Jesse and Cable told it straight, sheriff," the jowly bartender said, his voice quavering. "God, I swear I never seen a man that fast with a handgun, and I've seen 'em all in my time. I reckon this feller's even faster than Jesse here."

The young man called Jesse grinned. "I sure as hell don't intend to find out," he said. "Sheriff Bates, we all know Dolph was a friend of yours, but I'm telling you it was a fair fight. Now, if you want to take this man in, feel free. But don't count on any help from us."

The sheriff's weathered face colored slightly as he glanced around the room. He seemed to realize that not a man there would lend a hand—or shed a tear if one lawman came out on the messy end of a lead swap. Finally, Bates turned to Luther. "Let's hear your story, mister. From the top." He listened intently to Luther's account of the stolen mounts and his long ride from Kansas on the trail of the thieves. Luther didn't mention the shootings at the cabin. He didn't figure it had all that much to do with the story.

"So what do you plan to do now?" Bates asked as Luther finished his story. "You going after the rest of them?"

Luther shook his head. "The rest of the horses aren't my concern. They belong to somebody else. I got my horse back. That's what I set out to do."

Sheriff Bates sighed. "All right. That's the end of it then, I guess. For now." He turned to study Luther once more. "Mister, I don't know who you are, but there's something about you seems familiar. I suggest you ride out of my county before I get too curious."

"That's exactly what I had in mind, Sheriff Bates," Luther said as he turned toward the door. He strode outside, untied the black, and led the big mare toward the public stable two blocks away where Chili waited, rested and grained after the hard ride.

Jesse Evans leaned against the saloon doorway and watched the big man lead the black horse away. He smiled to himself as he heard the comments from inside; most of the voices were tinged with pure awe at what they had seen.

"Whoever he is," one voice said, "I sure wouldn't want to tangle with him. Fastest gun hand I've ever seen."

"Yeah," another added, "and I've got a suspicion he's just as good with a knife or his fists as he is with a gun. Did you see the size of that damn blade he's carrying?"

Jesse heard the old prospector Cable snort in derision. "He's more than that, boys. I seen that man before. Over to Denton, I seem to recall. Come face-to-face with Clay Allison. Backed old Clay plumb down."

"Aw hell, Cable," another voice said, "Clay Allison never backed down from no man in his life. Allison's an alligator, crazy to boot, and a top gun hand. No way he'd back down."

The clink of a bottle on glass sounded from Cable's table. "You take a good, long look at them eyes, boys? Cold as ice in a mountain blizzard. Well, I'm tellin' you, Clay Allison looked in 'em. And he didn't much like what he seen there. First time I ever seen Clay turn all meek and quiet. Like he was walkin' on eggs."

"Cable, you old coot," someone said, "your memory's got lighter than my money poke. I'd bet a week's pay that's the jasper that treed the Manning boys after they killed Dallas Stoudenmire down in El Paso."

"I'd take that bet, except you ain't had a real job in six months, Obie." It was the squeaky voice of the fat barkeep. "You listen to how he talked? Man's got some education, you can bet."

"Graduated from old Colonel Colt's shootin' college, that's for damn sure," Obie replied.

Jesse chuckled to himself. He suspected they were all dead wrong about the big man with the ice-blue eyes. Jesse had seen a lot of gunmen. He had ridden with Billy the Kid in the Lincoln County war and dodged more than a few lawmen himself. Odds were the man who killed Dolph Scarborough was on the run. Maybe from the law, maybe from something else. Jesse shrugged. It wasn't any of his affair.

He glanced toward the stable as the corral gate swung open and the big man, now mounted on the black, rode through, leading a leggy brown on a slack halter rein. The rider didn't dismount, but kneed the black into place and latched the gate from the saddle.

"Whoever you are, mister," Jesse muttered to the distant figure, "you're in a speck of trouble. You just killed Tyler Scarborough's little brother, and Tyler's not the kind to let that slide. You better ride with one eye on your back trail and your hand on that six-gun for a while—a long while."

Tyler Scarborough sat beside a small camp fire in a deep canyon in the Sangre de Cristos and stared at the spring wagon that had carried his brother's body from La Cueva.

Except for the hard set of stubbled jaw and smoldering violence that glittered in black eyes, few men would have recognized Tyler as the brother of the dead man in the wagon.

Tyler Scarborough was the physical opposite of Dolph. Tyler was short, barely five feet seven with his boots on, slightly built, clean-shaven except for a well-trimmed mustache almost as black as the eyes. The eyes and raven-black, collar-length hair were the legacy of their mother, a full-blood Choctaw. Tyler's cheekbones and nose also carried his mother's stamp; Dolph had taken most of his physical features—and his temper—from their Dutch-Irish trapper father. Tyler's hands were small, almost dainty, but they fit the bird's head grip of the .41 Colt Lightning carried high on his right hip.

Those who knew the brothers were aware of other differences as well, and all conceded that Tyler was the more dangerous of the two. All his life he had had to prove himself because of his size; the runt of the litter always had to fight harder for a place at the table, whether for food or respect. Tyler was the only man known ever to have whipped Dolph Scarborough in a fistfight or bettered him with rifle and handgun. Snakes came in all sizes, but the poison of the smaller one's bite was a lot more venomous in the Scarborough clan.

Tyler's eyes narrowed against the chilly mountain wind. He looked up from the flames to study the faces of the men who rode with him. Four were seated around the fire, sipping coffee or whiskey. Two more rode loose nighthawk duty, keeping an eye on the stolen horse herd to make sure the animals didn't drift too far from camp before sunup. Three more stood lookout in the rocks and crags of the canyon. There were still a few die-hard Apaches on the loose and plenty of outlaws in the rugged mountains that stretched south into Mexico. Outlaws weren't above stealing from other outlaws, Tyler knew. He had done it himself.

Another one of his men was still out scouting the country and was due back anytime. Dolph had made it an even dozen when he was alive.

The men in Tyler's gang were a rugged bunch, most of them unshaven and unwashed. The man sitting at his side was full-blood Apache. He was called Moondog because he saw visions of slavering wolves under a full moon during his peyote rites. Moondog was as dangerous with a knife as Tyler was with rifle and pistol, and if there was a better tracker in all of the Southwest Tyler had never seen him.

Carlos Vasquez sat next to Moondog. The burly, one-eyed Mexican was Tyler's number one lieutenant, the first to lead the charge to tree a town or drop a hammer on a bank teller or cowboy stupid enough to argue when the Scarborough bunch decided to take a horse herd. Vasquez wasn't long on smarts, but he was fearless, and he was loyal. He had ridden with Tyler for the last three years.

The others in the band were hard men, top shots with long gun or pistol, handpicked for their total disregard of human life and their preference for stealing instead of working for a living. Two had ridden with the Dolan-Murphy faction during the Lincoln County mess, two more were from the other side. Tyler didn't care who they had backed in that scrap. All that mattered was that they were his men now.

Moondog suddenly sat bolt upright, nostrils flaring as he tested the night air. "Company coming," he said.

Moments later a lookout called from his post along the canyon rim. "Bates on his way in!"

Tyler heaved himself to his feet and stared into the darkness until the sheriff rode through the tall, rustling pines into the camp clearing.

"It's about damn time you got here, Bates," Tyler groused. "You're three hours late."

Sheriff Ned Bates swung from his mount and massaged his saddle-sore backside. "Sorry, Tyler. Couldn't get here any sooner. I found you a buyer for those horses, though. He'll be here at first light, cash money in hand."

Tyler nodded, his expression grim. "How about the son of a bitch who killed Dolph?"

Bates shook his head. "Tracked him a good ways northeast. Lost the trail up by the Canadian River crossing. He's long gone by now, Tyler."

"Dammit, you should have locked the bastard up!"

Bates shrugged. "Legally, I had no grounds—"

"Since when," Tyler interrupted, "have you been so damn concerned about legalities? Legal never stopped you from taking my money. A man's on my payroll, Bates, I expect him to pull his weight."

"Come on, Tyler," Bates said, his voice almost a whine, "be reasonable. I have to put up a front for the voters. I get too far out of line, I'm out of office and we're out of business."

Tyler snorted in disgust. "I want that big man, Bates. I want his hide, a strip at a time—and, by God, I'll get it.

One way or another." He turned to the Apache at his side. "Moondog, go find out where the big bastard went. Soon as we get these horses sold, we'll head on up to Raton. Meet us there in four, five days."

The Apache nodded silently, gathered up his bedroll and saddlebags, and disappeared into the growing darkness.

"Can you trust Moondog to stay off the peyote, Tyler?" the sheriff asked.

"He'll stay off it. He doesn't have religious impulses when he's working." Tyler Scarborough sighed. "He knows I just buried my little brother, and I'm not in the mood to put up with any crap."

Ned Bates scrubbed a boot toe against the sandy soil. "Afraid I've got some more bad news for you, Tyler."

"*Now* what the hell?"

"Cattlemen's association has upped the ante on your head. You and your boys are worth anywhere from fifty to a couple hundred dollars apiece now."

Tyler snorted in disgust. "Nobody's got guts enough to come after that bounty."

"There's one man." Bates turned and stared off toward the southwest. "Word I got is that the association got the governor to pin a New Mexico marshal's badge on Pat Garrett. Told Garrett to put a posse together and run you boys down."

Tyler Scarborough mouthed a curse. Of all the men in New Mexico, Garrett was the last one he wanted to tangle with. The man was tough as rawhide and a bulldog on the trail. Worse than that, he knew how to pick men as tough as he was himself. "Where's Garrett now?"

"Down in White Oaks, from what I hear. Plans to make that sort of his base of operations." The sheriff snorted dust from his nostrils and wiped a sleeve across his nose. "The cowmen made it pretty clear, Tyler. They plan to run all the outlaws out of New Mexico."

Tyler swiped a hand across his chin, his brow wrinkled in thought. "Looks like we're going to have to find a new place to call home, then." He shrugged. "What the hell. Most of this country's rustled out, anyway. I think it's time to expand. Maybe take on Colorado, Kansas, Indian territory, the Texas panhandle. Lots of livestock and banks up that way."

Ned Bates sighed. "I guess it's the end of the trail for us, then."

Tyler shrugged. "Maybe not. I'll still need buyers for the stock, a contact with our Mexico traders, somebody to keep tabs on Garrett for me. I reckon I'll keep you on the payroll, Bates. I sort of like having a sheriff working for me."

The outlaw stared off into the distance for a moment. "Hell," he finally said with a snort, "even if Garrett wasn't on the prowl, I'd still go. There's a big bastard out there who gunned down my brother." Tyler's hand dropped to the grips of the .41 Lightning. "The son of a bitch will pay for that, Bates. He'll pay if it's the last thing I ever do."

CHAPTER
THREE

Luther McCall pulled the black to a stop on the north rim of Raton Pass, dismounted and loosened the saddle cinch, then turned to study his back trail.

It was a habit developed over years of drifting across the West, dodging lawmen and bounty hunters, one that had kept him from catching a slug between the shoulder blades on more than one occasion.

He listened to the labored breathing of the two horses as he stared back down the trail. The climb through the pass had winded both animals. Their nostrils flared and sides heaved as they gasped the thin mountain air back into tortured lungs.

The back trail was empty. Luther wasn't all that reassured. He couldn't shake the gnawing feeling that somebody or something was back there. He had been feeling that twitch in his gut for a day's ride. And a man who didn't trust his innards didn't last long out here.

Luther expected pursuit. A man didn't just ride into town, kill the brother of an outlaw gang leader, and simply ride away. The world wasn't that easy. There were hunters, and there were the hunted. Often, the roles reversed. Like now.

Luther wasn't particularly worried. The trail he had left was a convoluted one. It would take one hell of a good tracker to sort it out. And even if somebody did, it didn't matter much whether there was one man or a hundred after him. It only took one, if that one man happened to be good enough. Odds, Luther figured, were what a man made them. It was a simple philosophy, but one that kept a man's gut from eating him alive from the inside.

Satisfied that no one followed—at least close enough to see—and that the horses had their wind back, Luther tightened the cinch again and swung into the saddle. He tugged his hat down against the stiff wind that swirled from the southwest and compressed itself in the narrow pass, and touched spurs to the black's ribs.

He rode a wide circle around Raton. The town had a railroad, a telegraph office, and a sheriff with a reputation. Luther McCall didn't take any unnecessary chances. As he rode, the countryside gradually flattened, the mountain foothills giving way to rolling, rocky hills dotted with juniper and parched grass in need of rain.

The sun was nearing its midway point when the black stumbled and came up favoring a front leg. Luther stopped, swung down, and lifted the black's right front hoof. The steel shoe had worn through. A sliver of metal had snagged and peeled back away from the hoof. He patted the black's shoulder in reassurance, then reached for the big Damascus knife at his belt. He pried the remnants of the shoe from the hoof and tossed them aside. The black would have to be reshod before starting the long ride back to Kansas. If he decided to go back to Kansas. Luther was never sure exactly where he would be in a month's time.

He eased the horse's hoof back to the ground, stripped the saddle and equipment from the black, and transferred his tack to the leggy brown. There was no reason to make the black carry any extra weight. If the horse stepped on a sharp rock or stick and bruised the tender frog of the unprotected hoof, she could be crippled up for several days.

Chili walled his eyes, snorted, and humped his back as Luther stepped into the saddle, but soon settled down and gave up the idea of trying to buck Luther off. Luther chuckled at the antsy brown. He figured he and Chili were about even in the pitching department; half the time he could ride the brown through those bucking fits, half the time he couldn't. But the brown seemed to sense when it was time to work and time to play, and he seldom pitched except at playtime. Chili could be a pain in the butt, but the Tennessee-bred gelding had a lot of bottom. He could go all day on a cup of water and a handful of grass and still have some speed left if needed.

Luther tucked the black's lead rope under a cinch ring of the saddle, keeping his hands free to use a weapon if the need arose. He sat for a moment, thinking. The nearest blacksmith was in the little town of Cimarron. And Luther was more than a touch curious as to how the sandy-haired boy named Jimmy was making out. He hoped the boy was going to be all right. There was something about the kid that reminded Luther of his own childhood, when times had been better, before the troubles started. He felt something toward young Jimmy Macko that he hadn't felt in years. It took Luther a few minutes to identify the feeling. Then he realized it was a thin bond of friendship, a rare thing for a loner like himself to feel toward anyone.

"Ah, what the hell," he muttered aloud. He kneed the brown toward the breaks along the Cimarron River.

The sun sat on the lip of the western horizon as Luther rode into the small settlement in the bend of the river. The town looked even more deserted than it had just over a week ago when he had ridden out for New Mexico.

Here and there the lights of oil lanterns painted gold rectangles in windows as darkness began to fall on Cimarron. Luther paused at the edge of town long enough to satisfy himself that nothing unexpected lay ahead, then reined Chili toward the blacksmith shop at the west end of the street.

The shop was deserted, the forge cool to the touch. Luther was about to turn away when the door of a small adobe shack beside the shop swung open.

"Something I can do for you, mister?" The speaker was a short, stocky man, with no visible neck on thick, heavily muscled shoulders. He held a sourdough biscuit in one hand. The other hand rested at his belt buckle, close to the butt of an ancient Colt Dragoon percussion pistol.

"Are you the blacksmith?"

The man nodded. "Best one in town. Only one, for that matter. Got a problem?"

Luther nodded toward the black. The horse was busy scratching her ear against Chili's rump. "The black threw a shoe. Needs some new ones."

"Let's have a look." The blacksmith popped the last bite of biscuit into his mouth, strode to the black, ran a big but gentle hand along the horse's shoulder, and lifted a hoof. He glanced up at Luther. "Be tomorrow before I can do the job. Somewhere around noon. Got a buggy wheel to fix first. That all right with you?"

"Fine," Luther said. "Is there someplace around here I can leave the horses?"

The smith waved toward a small corral in back of the shop. A lean-to, barely visible in the growing darkness, stood along one side of the corral. "Got water and grain back there, hay if you want it. Have to charge you two bits for boarding the horses. Buck and a half for shoeing the black."

Luther dismounted. "Sounds fair enough."

The blacksmith reached for the reins. Luther shook his head. "I'll tend my own horses."

The burly man shrugged, then stared at Luther in the fading light. "I know you, mister," the blacksmith said.

Luther's muscles tensed.

"You're the fellow who brought little Jimmy Macko in here the other day."

"The same."

The blacksmith grinned. White teeth flashed against his sun-browned skin. "I thank you for that, mister. Jimmy's a good kid. Used to help me out around here some before his pa homesteaded that place out of town."

"How's Jimmy doing?"

The blacksmith's smile faded. "Hanging on. He's a tough youngster. Martha thinks he'll live if he makes it through the next couple of days." The blacksmith extended a big, callused hand. "George Winfield. Anybody helps Jimmy's a friend of mine."

Luther took the extended hand, felt the controlled power in the firm, dry palm and fingers. "I'm Travis."

Winfield seemed satisfied with that. He didn't press for any other details. "I like a man who tends his own mounts, Travis," the blacksmith said. "Some folks don't know horses need taking care of. Just ride 'em and put 'em up." He released Luther's hand and waved toward the corral.

"Feed's in the lean-to. Give em as much as you think they need. Won't change the price any."

The blacksmith lit a lantern and swung a creaky log gate open as Luther led the animals into the corral. He leaned against the fence as Luther stripped his tack from Chili, found a piece of burlap, and rubbed the animals down. "Is there a hotel in town?" Luther asked. "It's been a while since I've slept in a real bed."

"No hotel. Had one once, but it went out of business. Amy Caldwell's place is right across the street. Only two-story house in town. Sometimes she takes in a boarder, if the place isn't full. Not often it is. Good cook, clean rooms, and she's never overcharged anybody." Winfield fished a pipe from a shirt pocket, stuffed it, and fired it with a sulfur match as Luther finished tending his mounts and scooped a couple of double handfuls of grain into the feed trough. "Leave the saddle in the lean-to if you like," the blacksmith said. "Might want to keep those two rifles with you. Quiet town here, but sometimes good guns get stolen."

"Thanks. I intend to keep them handy."

"You planning to check in on Jimmy?"

"That's one of the reasons I came back to Cimarron. Thought I'd call on him in the morning."

Winfield drew at the pipe and nodded. "Good. I reckon he'll be right happy to see you, if he's awake." The blacksmith fell silent for a moment as Luther shouldered his saddlebags and tucked the Winchester and Sharps rifles under an arm. "I helped bury what was left of Jimmy's pa and uncle," Winfield finally said. "Worst job I ever had. Sure hope those bastards who killed 'em get what's coming to 'em."

"One has," Luther said. He made no attempt to explain the comment. The blacksmith didn't press for details, but his expression seemed to be one of satisfaction in the soft gold light from the lantern in his hand.

"Amy's place is right over there, Travis," Winfield said as the two strode from the corral. "Looks like she's still up. Light on in the window." He chuckled. "I wouldn't try to get fresh with that woman, by the way. Drummer came through here last winter. Tried to feel her up a bit. She whopped him in the head with a hot skillet and dusted his butt with birdshot when he run out the door."

Luther grinned to himself as the mental image formed in his mind. "I'll behave myself," he said.

He crossed the street and tapped on the door frame.

He wasn't prepared for the woman who answered the knock. Amy Caldwell was tall, blond, and full-bodied, with the erect posture of a proud and independent woman. Expressive dark blue eyes flecked with gold highlighted a serene, oval face. She wore a simple green housedress, but on her it looked as crisp and neat as a formal gown, Luther thought.

"Yes, sir? Something I can do for you?" Her voice was husky and musical, with a slight accent that seemed to hint at a European background.

"I'm looking for a room, ma'am," Luther said. "The black-smith said you might have one to rent for the night."

Amy Caldwell didn't answer for a moment. She stood in the doorway, her shoulder-length hair catching highlights from the lantern on the table nearby, and studied Luther as if trying to decide whether to admit the big man who carried an armful of rifles. Then she seemed to decide Luther was no threat. She nodded.

"I do. It isn't large, but it's comfortable. The charge is fifty cents a night. The price includes breakfast." The husky voice was solemn and businesslike. "I ask that you refrain from the use of tobacco or liquor in your room. And I request payment in advance."

The corners of Luther's mouth lifted in a slight smile. "That seems reasonable, ma'am." He drew a silver dollar from his pocket and handed her the coin. She swung the door open and motioned for him to enter.

Luther suddenly felt grubby from the accumulated trail grime and stubble as he stepped through the door. He wished he had taken the time to bathe and shave in one of the pools along the river. The room in which he stood was spotless. There were no traces of dust on the simple but sturdy furniture, and the hardwood floor—a rarity in small towns on the frontier—was polished to a smooth shine beneath his boots. The parlor was small, little more than ten by twelve feet, with a doorway to the right and a staircase to the left. A coatrack stood in a corner, a light blue shawl hanging on one hook and a new Stetson hat on another. At the side of the door, a double-barreled shotgun rested on pegs within easy reach.

"Your change, sir," Amy Caldwell said as she handed Luther two quarters. "Breakfast is at seven. For meals at other times, the café down the street serves an edible steak, despite the appearance of the establishment."

"That will be fine, ma'am," Luther said. The thought of a thick slice of beef made his mouth water. All he had eaten today was a couple of slabs of tough beef jerky and a few swallows from his canteen.

"If you will follow me, sir, I'll show you to your room." Amy Caldwell strode to the staircase and started to climb, firm hips swaying with each step. Luther understood why the drummer had made advances toward this strapping blond woman. He also remembered the hot frying pan and blast of birdshot. The image brought a wry smile to his lips. Amy Caldwell was definitely not a woman to fool with. She swung open the door at the top of the stairs and lit an oil lamp.

The room was small but sufficiently equipped. A full-sized bed rested against one wall. A water pitcher, bowl, and mirror stood on a shelf across from the bed, sharing space with a couple of folded towels. The room was at the corner of the building. A window framed by simple curtains stood open to catch the evening breeze. It also provided a good view of Cimarron's main street and the hills which bracketed the river.

"The outhouse is in the back," Amy Caldwell said casually, unembarrassed. "I hope this is satisfactory?"

Luther carefully propped the two rifles in a corner and turned to smile at the handsome blond woman. "It will do just fine, ma'am. Much better than what I'm accustomed to, in fact." He removed his hat and ran fingers through his chestnut-colored hair. "Is there a place in town where a man could get a bath? It would be a shame to waste clean sheets on all this trail dirt and sweat I'm carrying."

The woman raised an eyebrow. "I don't often have boarders who are overly concerned about their personal hygiene,

sir. I must say it's a pleasant surprise." She pursed her lips
in silent thought, then smiled. The lifting of full lips seemed
to bring a fresh light to her face. For the first time, Luther
noticed the thin sprinkle of freckles across the bridge of
her nose. The freckles added to her serene beauty.

"I'm afraid the barbershop is closed, sir. It's only open
two days a week," she said, "but I do have a tub in the
washroom behind the kitchen, if you don't mind bathing
in cold water. I've already banked the fire in the stove."

Luther smiled back. "I'm accustomed to cold water,
ma'am. A hot bath might be such a shock to the system
it would give me a case of the vapors."

Amy Caldwell laughed, her husky voice rising and falling like a musical instrument sliding through a scale. "We
couldn't have that. I must warn you the tub is rather small.
It will be a tight fit for a man your size."

"Ma'am, as grubby as I feel," Luther said, "I'll fit."

Two hours later Luther McCall sat in a chair by the
window of his room, freshly bathed and shaved and feeling
better than he had in days. He pondered the idea of going to
the cantina for a drink and a bite to eat, then abandoned the
notion. It wasn't worth the effort. He puffed out the lamp
and stood at the window, savoring the cool breeze as he
stared into the darkness. The moon had not yet risen, and
a slight haze filtered out most of the starlight.

His eyes narrowed as a light flickered on the side of a
hill in the distant river breaks. A camp fire, most likely.
He watched for several minutes until the small light winked
out. No need to get twitchy, he scolded himself. Could be
anybody out there. Sheepherder, hunter, even a cowboy
riding drift. Not everybody in the world is after your hide.
Still, he pushed the chair closer to the bed and draped his
gun belt over it, keeping the weapon within easy reach as
he stretched out on the soft mattress. Being twitchy was one
thing. Not being ready for anything that might happen was
just plain dumb.

The sun was perched atop the thin steeple of the whitewashed
church when Luther stepped from the boardinghouse and
surveyed the main street of Cimarron.

The morning air was still and comfortably cool. Soon, Luther knew, the temperature would start to climb, and by midday any exposed iron would fry a man's hand at the touch. At the moment he didn't care. His belt was stretched almost to the breaking point from the heavy table Amy Caldwell set for breakfast. Luther couldn't remember the last time he'd had such a good meal. Amy Caldwell was a fine cook, and she didn't skimp on the servings.

Cimarron was beginning to stir, but the town seemed to be one that awakened slowly, like a gambler after a good night's run of whiskey and cards.

The tall man with the potbelly swept a worn-down broom over the narrow porch of the mercantile store. A couple of old-timers wandered from the unmarked two-room adobe café, settled down on a bench by the door, and reached for chewing tobacco. The cantina's door was closed. It was too early in the day for civilized men to drink.

A young, clean-shaven cowboy rode past, nodded a silent greeting to Luther, and reined his mount to a stop at the general store hitch rail. Maybe the man at the camp fire last night, Luther thought. The lean cowboy seemed to pose no threat.

Luther heard the whoosh of the bellows and crackle of kindling as the blacksmith fired up his forge. At least there was one man who believed in getting an early start, Luther mused. A spring buggy, worn and badly in need of paint and pulled by an aging, swaybacked gray mare came into view. The couple on the buggy seat looked as worn and tired as the mare. They were stooped and weathered, in the sunset of their years. The town was quiet and peaceful. Most of the residents he'd seen didn't even carry guns.

Luther suddenly noticed something that had escaped him in his earlier visit to Cimarron. There were few kids about. No sign of a school building. And almost no people between the age of fourteen and thirty. That didn't seem right, somehow. A town should have kids. They added a little spirit to a place. A few skinned knees and dirty faces and noisy games brightened up a town. Maybe that was one reason Jimmy Macko had so many friends among the adults.

Luther saw nothing out of the ordinary, no apparent danger, no one who didn't seem to belong. Except for the older population and the lack of young people, Cimarron could have been the settlement in Nebraska that had been the closest thing Luther had ever had to a hometown. There he had found a new world, one more pleasant than reality. He had found the world of books in the little one-room school. The discovery had saved his sanity on more than one long and boring ride through the vast, empty lands of the West. It also triggered in Luther an insatiable appetite for learning. Most people were startled to learn that a man who looked like a threadbare drifter most of the time could discuss Aristotle or Shakespeare with as much ease as he argued the merits of various horses or weapons.

He had noticed a small, glass-fronted case in the corner of Amy Caldwell's dining room this morning. Behind the glass were a dozen or more books, all with the appearance of heavy use. It was something he intended to ask Amy about before taking his leave of Cimarron.

Out of habit more than anything else, Luther flicked the hold-down thong from the hammer of the Colt on his hip and loosened the weapon in the holster before stepping into the street. He carried the Winchester in his left hand, the metal of the receiver cool and reassuring to the touch.

He strode past the two old-timers lounging outside the café and nodded a greeting. The action went unanswered; the old men stared silently and suspiciously as Luther walked past.

A few minutes later Luther tapped at the door of the marshal's home beside the church. The door creaked open.

"Oh, it's you," Josh Turlock said by way of greeting. "Never thought we'd see you again in these parts." The marshal's tone seemed to imply that he would have been just as happy not to have seen Luther again.

"How's Jimmy?"

Turlock shrugged. "Holding his own. Barely. Martha seems to think he's going to make it."

"Can I see him?"

"Take it up with the boss," Turlock said. "Martha," he called over his shoulder, "man here to see Jimmy."

Martha Turlock wiped her hands on her apron as she stepped to the open door. "Mr. Travis," she said, a smile creasing her broad face, "it's good to see you again." She glanced toward the interior of the house. "Jimmy's asleep again—or unconscious, it's hard to tell which. I'd rather you didn't disturb him at the moment, but please come in. I've got a fresh pot of coffee brewing."

Luther glanced at the marshal. Josh Turlock didn't seem overly pleased at his wife's invitation, but he stepped aside and waved for Luther to enter.

The house had the look and smell of a real home, Luther thought as he put the Winchester on a rack beside an ancient Yellow Boy .44 rimfire rifle. He removed his hat. "Thank you, Mrs. Turlock," he said. "How is Jimmy doing?"

Martha frowned. "I can't be sure. He lost so much blood, poor thing. But he's a fighter. His fever's down, and there's no sign of infection. The next day or so will make the difference. Have a seat, Mr. Travis. I'll get some coffee."

Luther pulled out a chair and sat at a sturdy, worn table. Josh Turlock sat across from him, a frown on the weathered face, and studied Luther with more intensity than was comfortable.

Martha placed a mug of steaming coffee before each of the men. "Thank you, ma'am," Luther said. He glanced at the wide face and noticed the red streaks in the whites of the green eyes. Martha Turlock looked harried and worn. Luther figured she hadn't had more than a couple of hours' sleep a day since he had brought the wounded boy here.

"Milk or sugar?" Martha asked.

Luther shook his head. "No, thank you, Mrs. Turlock. I'll drink it just the way the Creator intended."

Martha brought her own mug over and sat at Luther's left. "Mr. Travis, it would be best if you didn't see Jimmy right now. He needs his rest."

Luther nodded. "I understand, ma'am."

Martha sipped at her coffee and peered across the lip of the mug. "If you had been a half hour later arriving at the cabin, Mr. Travis, Jimmy would have been dead for certain. I'm curious about something, though. Where did you learn to make the Cheyenne medicine poultice?"

"From an old Cheyenne healer," Luther said. "I spent some time with the Southern Cheyenne once. Their healers may not know much of modern medicine, Mrs. Turlock, but some of the old ways have astounding properties." He sipped at his own mug. "How did you recognize the poultice? Very few people outside the tribe know of it."

Martha half smiled, a tired expression. "My mother was half Cheyenne." Luther heard the note of pride in her tone. "In her time she was as famous a healer as any medicine man in the tribe. I've used that poultice before myself, when I can find the right plants and herbs. And you're right. It does have almost magical qualities."

A momentary hush fell over the table. Martha's eyelids fluttered and almost closed. The poor woman's almost out on her feet, Luther thought. She must be totally exhausted.

Josh Turlock broke the silence. "Mind telling me where you've been the last few days, Travis?"

Luther leveled a steady gaze at the marshal. "Yes, as a matter of fact, I do," he said calmly. "It was personal business."

Turlock's nostrils flared in a silent snort. "Whatever you say. Staying long?"

Luther felt the irritation begin to build in his gut. "Haven't decided, Marshal," he said.

"Might be best if you drifted on."

Luther struggled to keep a rein on his often short temper. "Are you telling me to leave town, Marshal?"

Turlock held Luther's stare without blinking. "Not exactly. As long as you don't break the law in my town, I've got no reason to run you out. We don't get many strangers here, Travis. But there's been talk."

"There's always talk, Marshal Turlock." Luther's voice went cold. He continued to glare into the marshal's deep hazel eyes. He saw no fear there. This old man may just be tougher than he looks, Luther thought. "After I'm sure Jimmy's going to be all right, maybe I'll move on."

"Whatever." Turlock's voice was flat, without expression.

"Josh Turlock, you cranky old coot," Martha gently scolded, "this man is a guest in our house. If you want to play lawman, go outside to play." She turned to Luther. "You come back tomorrow, Mr. Travis. If Jimmy's awake, I'm sure he will be glad to see you."

Luther drained the last of his coffee, pushed away from the table, and stood. "Thank you, ma'am. I appreciate it. And thank you for the coffee."

He retrieved his rifle and hat and strode outside. Josh Turlock followed, the clack of his cane distinct on the worn floor. The door closed with a soft thump behind them.

"Travis," Turlock said as he reached for his pipe, "you don't seem to be the fatherly type to me."

"I'm not. But I like that boy, Marshal. You aren't going to tell me I can't see him, are you?"

Josh Turlock grinned around the pipe stem. "Martha said you could see him. I'm not about to get that woman riled up. Might as well take a bite of the end of a forty-four and pull the trigger." He scratched a match and fired the pipe.

Luther touched fingers to his hat brim and strode away. He could feel the marshal's gaze on the center of his back, a small cold spot. His anger at the lawman began to fade, replaced by a grudging admiration. *I don't think I want to cross blades with that old man,* Luther thought.

CHAPTER FOUR

Luther sat at a wobbly corner table in the one-room cantina, nursing a pleasantly cool beer as he waited for the blacksmith to finish putting new shoes on the black mare.

His irritation with the marshal had faded as the sun passed the midday point. It had been a quiet morning in Cimarron. Almost boring, in fact. But Luther still couldn't put down the uneasy feeling in his gut after spotting that distant camp fire in the hills the evening before.

He had saddled the brown and ridden out to check the site. The tracks were plain enough. Someone had camped out there, someone who left the distinctive imprint of Apache-style moccasins behind. The ashes of the small fire were cold; a night beetle's track crossed one of the moccasin prints. The beetle tracks told Luther that whoever had been there had not stayed long. The bugs only moved in the hours between midnight and sunrise. The hoofprints around the camp were those of a shod horse, and Apaches seldom bothered to put iron on their horses' feet. The odd combination nagged at Luther. He had trailed the horseman for a couple of hours. The tracks led toward Raton. Luther couldn't dismiss the notion that maybe the trail passed through Raton and on to La Cueva.

Maybe it didn't mean anything, but Luther wasn't going to bet his life on it. He would keep a sharp eye out until he rode out of Cimarron.

He sipped at the beer and sighed in satisfaction. Cimarron's cantina wasn't the cleanest place Luther had ever been in, but the beer was top quality. Not the rank home brew or watered-down beer of most frontier towns, but a smooth, light pilsner whose bubbles stirred a rich but delicate flavor of hops and the slightest hint of barley and malt. Luther hadn't tasted a better beer since he'd stopped off in Fredericksburg several months back. Those Fredericksburg Germans knew their brew, and this one had a distinct German touch.

The thought brought his mind back to Amy Caldwell. It was a short trip.

He had been right about the accent. She was the second American-born generation of a German immigrant family. He hadn't been able to get much more than that from her. A pompous, paunchy cattle buyer wearing a silk vest and forty dollar handmade boots had dominated the breakfast conversation, obviously trying to impress Amy with his money and influence. Luther could see it wasn't working. The amused tolerance in the blonde's blue eyes told Luther that Amy wasn't the sort to be impressed by braggarts and men who thought they were bigger than they really were. Maybe he would have a chance to talk more with Amy at supper time—or dinner, as she preferred to call it.

Luther wasn't sure why he had such an interest in Amy Caldwell. He was no ladies' man, never had tried to be. And he would be moving on in a couple of days, as soon as he got to visit with Jimmy and make sure the boy would recover. Luther wasn't in the market for a personal relationship with a woman, anyway. He didn't have anything to offer, especially a future, given the trails he rode. But there was something special about Amy Caldwell.

He glanced up as the blacksmith strode into the cantina, rubbing a fresh bruise on a thick forearm. Winfield grinned a greeting to Luther. "Black's ready," he said. "Not the easiest horse I ever shod. The ornery devil kicked the bejesus out of me a couple times."

Luther nodded. "The black's a handful sometimes," he said, "but you haven't had real fun until you try to tack shoes on that brown of mine." Luther dug into a pocket and sorted out the payment due the blacksmith. "Buy you a beer as a bonus for wrestling her," he said.

The blacksmith shook his head. "Thanks for the offer, but I've got a couple more jobs to get done this afternoon."

He pocketed the coins without counting them. "Going to be staying around long, Travis?"

Irritation warmed Luther's gut again. He was getting a little tired of people prying into his personal affairs. But he heard no implied threat in the blacksmith's tone. "I'm not sure yet."

"Well, good luck to you, Travis. See you around." The blacksmith turned and strode from the cantina.

"Another beer, mister?" The cantina owner, a wiry former cowboy with bushy gray eyebrows and a mop of unruly silver hair, gestured toward Luther's almost empty mug.

"No, thanks," Luther said. "I have some things to do. You serve a fine brew. Best I've had since Fredericksburg."

The old-timer smiled. "Good to have someone in who appreciates a good beer. Most of the cowboys who come in wouldn't know the difference between pilsner and mule piss."

Luther nodded a farewell to the cantina owner and stepped into the street. The strong southwest wind was like a blast from a smelting furnace. Blowing dust eddied along the street, ruffled the beards and scattered the pile of whittling chips produced by the two old men who still sat in front of the small café. The two watched in silent curiosity as Luther strode past.

Over the moan of the wind, Luther heard one of the old men comment, "Gunfighter, sure as I'm sittin' here. Bounty hunter, maybe."

"Nah," the other muttered. "That jasper's on the run. Tell by the way he's all the time watchin' for somethin'."

The voices faded as Luther walked on, a wry smile on his lips. Cimarron was a decent enough town, but it sure had its share of nosy people, he mused. At least as long as they're guessing, he thought, they don't know anything for sure. And that's the way I plan to keep it. After another day or so it wouldn't matter. Luther McCall would be long gone from Cimarron.

Tyler Scarborough was in a foul mood.

The price for the stolen horses had been five dollars a head less than he had expected. He'd taken part of the loss out of Ned Bates's share. That should teach the damn badge toter to bring a better buyer next time.

There hadn't been time to find another buyer. There was still a big man on a brown horse out there somewhere. He owed it to Dolph to handle that problem first. And Hoss Duggan had ridden back in, his scout to the south complete, and confirmed what Bates had reported. Pat Garrett was in White Oaks recruiting men to hunt outlaws. That meant it was going to get hot for men in Tyler's business damn fast in northern New Mexico. Getting to where a man can't make a decent living these days, Tyler groused to himself.

Tyler squatted beside the banked ashes of the camp fire and glared up at the swarthy Apache standing before him. "You sure that bastard's in Cimarron, Moondog?"

The Apache's expression didn't change. "Saw him. He's there. Spent the night in a house on the edge of town."

Tyler glanced at Carlos Vasquez. The burly, one-eyed Mexican drained the last of a half-pint of mescal, wiped a hand across his lips, and grinned at Tyler. "Want to go get the son of a bitch, boss?" Vasquez asked.

"Could be a bigger chore than it looks," Moondog said. His black eyes were without expression in the mahogany face. "This man knows how to hide a trail. He's damn sure good enough with a gun. Dolph found that out. Maybe he's got friends in Cimarron."

Tyler snorted in disgust, then rose. "Bunch of old farts and a few women. They won't fight. Haven't got the guts— wait a minute." He snapped his fingers at the sudden thought. "Cimarron's got everything we need. No law except an old crippled town marshal. It's in a territory, not an organized county. It's a no-man's-land, close enough to New Mexico that we could keep using our contacts here but still stay outside Garrett's jurisdiction." Tyler's bleak mood began to lift as he warmed to the idea. "Boys, if we had Cimarron, we could raid north into Kansas and Colorado, south into Texas—hell, we could go anywhere and do anything we wanted. We'd be rich men in a couple of years."

Carlos Vasquez's one good eye narrowed. The Mexican showed no effects from the half-pint of mescal he'd downed in the last hour and a half. "What you got in mind, boss?"

Tyler Scarborough grinned. "We need a new hideout anyway. By God, that's what we'll do. We'll tree the damn town. Take over Cimarron, lock, stock, and hound dog. Men in our business couldn't ask for a better Robber's Roost."

Vasquez flashed a quick smile, revealing a gap where a front tooth had been. "Don't see why not." He rubbed a hand on the worn leather of the shotgun-style leggings he wore. "Hell, it'd be better than Hole in the Wall. Damn sight more comfortable anyway. Let's ride."

Tyler raised a hand. "Rein in a minute, Vasquez. We'll need supplies to last a spell. I doubt there's enough ammunition and grub in Cimarron to hold an outfit like this more than a couple of days. We'll stop in La Cueva and stock up." His brow furrowed as his mind raced, figuring the angles. Taking the town wouldn't be that hard. But some serious planning had to be done first.

In the meantime, there was the big man. He was a debt that had to be collected while the chips were still on the table. Besides, Tyler would just as soon have the stranger out of the way before he and his men rode into Cimarron. That man was the only serious gun in the little town. One of the secrets of success in the outlaw business was to think things through and not get careless. Dolph had been careless, and it had gotten him dead. He should have watched his back trail.

Tyler made up his mind. He'd have to take first things first. "Hoss!" he yelled.

Hoss Duggan ambled up a moment later, gnawing on a cold biscuit. Duggan was tall, better than six feet four, lean and wiry, and one of the best hands in the bunch when it came to handguns. "Yeah, Tyler?"

"Catch a fresh horse. I want you to slip into Cimarron and put a bunch of holes in that bastard who shot Dolph." He went over the description of the big man again to refresh Hoss's memory. Duggan wasn't as quick upstairs as he was with a pistol. "I'd rather do it myself," Tyler concluded, "but I got some planning to do. We're short of cash. I've got to figure a couple of things we can do quick after we take over Cimarron."

Duggan finished the biscuit and wiped a big hand over the heavy stubble on his face. "We could borrow a few of these New Mexico cows on the way out. Probably find a buyer easy enough up in Indian territory."

Tyler waved off the suggestion. "I don't want to give Garrett any reason to follow us. You just leave the thinking to me, Hoss. Go kill a man."

Duggan stroked the butt of the Colt on his hip lovingly. "Glad to," he said. He turned and strode toward the band's horse remuda grazing about a hundred yards away.

Tyler watched the tall man catch a big, rangy roan, saddle up, and ride off toward the northeast. He would rather have sent Moondog. The Apache would have brought the big man's scalp and ears back for sure, and probably so quietly that nobody would ever know about it. But Hoss Duggan was more expendable if something went wrong; if Duggan didn't come back, it was no big loss. Tyler wanted Moondog and Vasquez at his stirrup. The Apache and the one-eyed Mexican were good-luck charms as far as Tyler was concerned.

Tyler waited until the horseman disappeared over the valley ridge, then turned to Vasquez. "Let's break camp, Carlos," he said. "I'd like to be in La Cueva before sundown."

"Me too, boss," Vasquez said with a leer. "Got that itch that says I need me a señorita." The Mexican chuckled aloud. "Man can't tree a town right without gettin' his milk drained first. La Cueva's the place to get that done." Vasquez turned away and began issuing orders to break camp.

Tyler glanced at the Apache. "How about you, Moondog? You got that itch, too?"

The Apache shook his head, his shoulder-length black hair rippling in the breeze. "No woman. Peyote tonight. Better than woman, anyway. Woman can't bring medicine vision." Moondog reached for his tobacco sack and expertly rolled a cigarette. He dropped the pidgin English act that he sometimes put on for Tyler's amusement. "Still thinking about that bank up in Trail City?"

Tyler smiled. "Damned if sometimes you don't just flat read my mind, Moondog. That place'll be bulging with money by the dark of the moon. And by then we'll own us a town. When we get set up at Cimarron, by God, nobody'll be able to dig us out. Those old farts up there don't know it, but that town can be turned into a damned fortress."

Moondog took a long drag on the cigarette, his gaze drifting toward the horizon. "There's one man there who could maybe see that." Moondog's voice was soft against the rustle of windblown grass and trees. "What if Hoss can't put him down?"

"Then the whole bunch of us ride him down," Tyler said, the tightness of anger back in his voice. "I don't care how good he is, he can't take a dozen top gun hands."

Moondog exhaled through his nostrils. "Maybe, maybe not. I got a feeling this man may be one tough piñon nut. Let's be careful we don't break a tooth on him."

Luther McCall leaned back in his chair and sighed in contentment. The Cimarron café was small, barely able to accommodate a half dozen people at a time. The walls and single window were stained with years of grime and cooking grease smoke, but the steak was top drawer. Just goes to show a man can't always judge quality by appearance, he mused. He rose, picked up the Winchester, paid his bill, and stepped outside. The sun was near the western horizon, the street deserted as the day wound down.

He strode toward Amy Caldwell's boardinghouse, the faint click and jingle of coins in his pocket reminding him that he was running short of cash a lot sooner than he'd planned. Getting the black shod and himself and the horses boarded, fed, and groomed for two days and nights had taken a sizeable bite from a poke that had been slim to start with. But, he reminded himself, it didn't matter. He had enough left to buy some trail supplies, and tomorrow he'd be moving out. A man didn't need much cash where there were no places to spend it.

He glanced over his shoulder toward the house beside the white church. He had asked about Jimmy earlier in the afternoon. Martha Turlock seemed more confident now that the boy would soon be out of danger. He might even be awake tomorrow, Martha figured. Luther was beginning to get twitchy being in town. He was like the antsy brown gelding. He and Chili were both more comfortable on the trail. Towns had too many ways to spring surprises on a man.

Amy Caldwell sat at a table in the small parlor, an oil lantern casting a weak yellow glow over the book opened before her. She glanced up and smiled a greeting.

Luther placed his hat on a peg. The Stetson was no longer there. The cattle buyer had moved out on the weekly mail stage before noon. Luther nodded toward the open book. "Mind if I ask what you're reading, ma'am?"

"*The Divine Comedy*. By Dante."

Luther smiled. "I still haven't quite grasped what Dante was trying to tell us with the first level of the descent. I've been to Purgatory myself—the one in Colorado. From what I saw in Colorado, I'm not too sure they're much different."

Amy raised a surprised eyebrow. "You read Dante?"

"Sometime back. I was under a bit of a handicap, though. The copy I had was in Italian. I'm still trying to learn that language."

"Mr. Travis, you are a man of some surprises," Amy said. She tapped a finger on one of the pages. "Perhaps you can enlighten me. I'm a bit confused about Beatrice in *la Divina Commedia*. I get the feeling there was more to her than Dante put down in ink."

Luther stroked his thick mustache in thought. "I believe Beatrice really existed. I had a long talk with an old trapper once, during a cold winter in the Grand Tetons. The old man was convinced Beatrice was a real girl, name of Beatrice Portinari. Dante wanted her, but couldn't have her. He used her as the somewhat idealized model for the Beatrice in the book."

Amy studied Luther's face for a moment, her full lips pursed in concentration. "That could explain a lot of things— oh, excuse me, Mr. Travis. Please, have a seat. I was about to pour a glass of wine. Would you care to join me?"

"Thank you, ma'am."

She smiled softly. "If we're going to be discussing the classics of literature, Mr. Travis, why don't you just call me Amy?"

"If you'll drop the 'mister' and just call me Travis."

Amy left the room for a moment, then returned with a bottle of white wine and a pair of almost dainty, long-stemmed wine glasses. Luther stood until she had uncorked the wine and poured a generous amount in both glasses, then took a seat a respectful distance from her chair.

"Tell me more about Dante and Beatrice, Travis," Amy said. "This is the first opportunity I've had to discuss something besides horses, cattle, and the weather in years."

Luther sipped at the wine. It was cool, dry, soothing to the palate, with a gentle bouquet. "It's very good," he said. "German? Rhine Valley?"

Amy smiled again. The whole room seemed to brighten. "And all this time I thought Western men appreciated nothing but straight bourbon. You surprise me again, Travis. It's Rhine Valley, true. Straight from the old country. One of my few but savored weaknesses." She sipped at her glass and sighed. "Now, back to this theory of unrequited love and an Italian poet."

Luther swirled the wine and peered over the glass at the blond woman. "This old trapper was sure Dante loved Beatrice, and when she married someone else and then died in the year 1290, Dante was devastated by grief. That's why Dante used her as the model for Beatrice. I think the old-timer was right. All I've read about Dante since seems to support the idea."

"Yes, that would explain the lofty level to which he has raised Beatrice in the *Comedy*," Amy said. "What happened to him after she died?"

Luther sipped at the wine, savored the soft touch of the liquid on his tongue, and sighed. "If I'm not mistaken, Dante got caught up in political intrigue. On the losing side, as it turned out. He was never able to return to Florence. He spent the rest of his life wandering about."

Amy raised an eyebrow. "Not to be impertinent, Travis, but a wanderer something like yourself?"

"I'd like to think so," he said thoughtfully, "but I'm afraid the reason for my wandering has different roots."

"I'm sorry. Excuse me for prying into something that is none of my business. It just slipped out. It won't happen again."

Luther flashed a quick smile. "I wish everyone in Cimarron was as understanding, Amy. Now, what's your theory on the meaning of the first level of the descent?"

The distant bong of a mantel clock in the dining room jarred Luther. It was eleven o'clock; he hadn't realized so much time had passed. But then, it had been a long time since he had been involved in a discussion of classical literature with a pretty woman. He stood. "It's late, Amy. I'm sorry to have kept you up so long."

"Nonsense, Travis. I've had a marvelous time. I feel more awake and alive now than I have in months. Thank you."

"It was my pleasure." Reluctantly, Luther started for the stairs.

"Travis? Anytime you wish to borrow one of the books from my rather modest library, please feel free to do so."

He glanced back at the blond woman beside the table, unsure if the warmth he felt came from the wine or something else. He suspected the latter. He shook his head. "Thanks for the offer, but I'll be moving on soon. Probably tomorrow, after I get to see Jimmy."

"Oh. I see." Luther thought he detected a note of regret in Amy's voice.

Half an hour later, Luther lay stretched out on the bed, listening to the night sounds.

An owl hooted from somewhere along the tree-lined river and fell silent, waiting for a reply. A mockingbird sang from a nearby cottonwood. Luther didn't know why the birds often sang throughout the night, and he didn't care. It was enough that they felt the need. It was better entertainment than a full band of human musicians.

A coyote wailed from the hills behind the town. Luther smiled as the mournful cry drifted thin and lonely on the light westerly breeze. He had always felt a kinship with the coyote. They were loners most of the time, scroungers, living off the land. Cursed, hunted, and shot at by the white man, but celebrated for their wit and wisdom in stories told by almost all Plains Indian tribes. The coyote's cry set off a yapping of the town dogs, eager to take up the chase if the wild animal came too close to their homes. That's the way it usually is, Luther mused; the wild, free things are hated and hunted by those whose boundaries are measured by fences, roads, and artificial barriers made by man.

Most times, the coyote's wail was a beckoning cry to Luther, a call to share the wilderness of the vast prairies and rugged mountains of the West. But tonight, it triggered a feeling Luther had almost forgotten.

Loneliness.

Luther tried to brush the feeling aside. He knew the seeds of the quiet ache. They had been planted over wine and conversation with an attractive woman during the last few hours. *It's time to move on, McCall,* he admonished himself. *Amy Caldwell is starting to get under your skin. And that's something neither of you can afford.*

Gradually the coyote's moans faded to a broken whimper and stopped.

The Apache called Moondog sat cross-legged in the center of a circle of fist-sized medicine stones, hands resting on his thighs, palms up, and stared at the blanket of stars above the western horizon.

He had chosen the site with care for the peyote rites. The bald sandstone rock at the top of the hill was four miles from the town called Raton. From its crest, the visions could come without obstruction from any of the four winds. The still night air smelled of juniper and pine. There was no moon. Each star stood out in sharp relief as the peyote buttons released their vision power in his belly.

A sudden streak of light flashed across the western sky and fell behind the distant mountains. The brief flare revealed a lone figure on horseback. Though the distance was great, Moondog saw the rider clearly. The man was tall and strong, astride a painted horse. The sky behind the rider brightened into streaks of gold and red. The sun colors. The horseman clutched a rifle in one hand, its muzzle pointed toward the sky, the butt resting on a muscular thigh. A fresh scalp fluttered in an unfelt wind from the fore stock of the rifle. The horseman raised the weapon above his head in a silent salute, then reined the spotted horse about. Moondog watched as the vision of the proud Apache warrior seemed to fade. The horse and rider slowly dissolved, like a dirt clod in a gently flowing stream, and finally disappeared.

Moondog waited. The vision had been good. It spoke of the days of his ancestors, when the Apache ruled the Southwest. It spoke of the bravery of his father and his father's father. Moondog felt the ghost warrior's power pump through his veins and flow into his forearms, his thighs, and was content.

His stomach gurgled as it digested the peyote buttons. Soon the medicine purge would come. Moondog felt the sweat bead across his forehead and upper lip.

The second vision grew from the north. A fat, round moon lifted quickly into the sky, bathing the medicine hill in a pure, white light. Clouds wisped across the face that peered down from the large round world above.

The first flutters of unease rippled through Moondog's gut, grew quickly into a sense of foreboding and dread. Then the monster came—huge, powerful, its broad chest heaving, eyes a foot apart glowing red against black fur, foam dripping from massive jaws that gaped open to show sharp, jagged fangs. The beast moved its head slowly, every motion in sharp relief as it stood before the huge moon. It stared at the man in the circle of stones for several heartbeats. Then the beast stalked toward the circle, dragging the moon behind it. Fear grew to all-consuming terror in Moondog's chest; he was unable to move, even to cry out, as the shaggy beast stopped just outside the holy circle. The great head moved slowly from side to side, but the fiery eyes never strayed from Moondog's face. From the depths of each red pupil a yellow spark formed and grew. Moondog could only watch in horror as the sparks built in fury, then stabbed out like the explosion of a pine knot in a camp fire. The twin sparks flashed through the circle of stones. Moondog felt the pain of searing heat as the sparks bored into his left breast. Then the great, slavering jaws pulled back, carrying the moon with them; the figures of wolf and moon sped away, grew small in the distance, and vanished in a quick shower of sparks.

Darkness fell again on the circle of medicine stones. Moondog felt the sweat pour down his face, smelled the powerful scent of fear from his own body. His bladder had loosened under the wrenching terror. Then the purge began. His stomach convulsed, spewing the remnants of the peyote buttons before him.

Moondog knelt and gasped for air as the convulsions finally stopped. The terror remained. Each time the Moon Wolf had appeared to him in a vision, the hot sparks from the eyes had touched someone. The sparks were the message of death. Moondog shuddered violently.

The Moon Wolf had touched him.

He pulled his shirt aside and glanced at his breast. Two small red spots on his skin had already begun to blister. Moondog knew then he was going to die.

The Moon Wolf had spoken.

CHAPTER
FIVE

Luther McCall squatted beside the small cot in the back room of the Turlock home and smiled at the pale, wan face of the boy on the cot.

Jimmy Macko was still a mighty sick young man and in considerable pain, but it looked to Luther like the boy was on the way back. The fever was gone now, the smooth cheeks and forehead free of sweat. The fresh bandage across his shoulder and back showed no signs of blood. And Martha Turlock had said there was no indication of blood poisoning. Martha waited in the front room while Luther visited; he hoped she was taking the opportunity to catch a quick nap. The woman was obviously exhausted.

"How're you doing, Jimmy?" Luther asked.

The boy's eyes were bright with pain, but there were no tears on his cheeks. "Hurting some." The voice was thin and shaky. Luther had to lean forward to hear clearly. "But Aunt Martha says it won't be so bad tomorrow."

"I didn't know she was your aunt."

"She's not, really. But she's the closest thing I've got to a relative now. Besides, everybody calls her Aunt Martha." The boy winced at a fresh stab of pain from the torn muscles. "She likes to be called that."

"She's a nice woman, Jimmy. I like her." Luther sighed quietly; it was as if a heavy weight had been lifted from his shoulders. He had worried more about the boy than he wanted to admit. For a man who tries his damnedest to avoid making friends, McCall, he scolded himself, you're getting awful attached to some folks here in Cimarron.

"Did—did you get your horse back?"

The question caught Luther by surprise. Despite his own pain and loss, Jimmy Macko still remembered the horse. For some reason Luther felt a tightness in his throat. "Yes, Jimmy. I got her back."

The boy nodded weakly. "That's good. Did you kill those men who—who burned up Pa and Uncle Ed?" There was a hopeful note in the trembling voice.

"Just one of them. The one who was riding my horse." Luther pondered for an instant how he could explain to the boy that the other men weren't his concern, that Luther McCall was no avenging knight on a white horse.

"Good. I'm glad you got him." A tint of anger and determination strengthened the youth's voice. "I'll get the others. When I'm well."

Luther nodded. "I wouldn't be a bit surprised if you did, Jimmy." Once again he saw a bit of himself reflected in the pale twelve-year-old face. Luther McCall had made the same vow as a youngster, only a little older than Jimmy, and he had made it stick. He had extracted his own justice from the men who killed his father. Vengeance had come with a price. But Luther was willing to pay.

Jimmy fell silent for a moment, his breathing shallow but regular. "Aunt Martha says your name's Mr. Travis. I guess I didn't ask before."

Luther smiled. "You had other things on your mind then, Jimmy. You can drop the 'mister.' Just call me Travis." Luther knew he should be going now. The boy needed rest; even the effort of talking was taking its toll. But Luther had to admit he was reluctant to leave. This would probably be the last time he ever saw Jimmy Macko. One day their trails might cross again, if they both lived, but the West was a big country.

"Travis? Would you do me a favor?" Jimmy's eyelids lowered some. The boy was fighting sleep, even though it would be an escape from the pain.

"Sure, Jimmy."

"Aunt Martha . . . put my rifle in the corner over there. I can't reach it from here."

Luther retrieved the Remington .22 from the far corner and leaned it against the wall beside Jimmy's bed. "A weapon won't do a man much good if he can't reach it. Is there anything else you need?"

The boy's face twisted as a new stab of pain wracked his thin body. The grimace quickly passed. "I just have one shell for the rifle. Could you loan me some more?"

Luther raised his opinion of Jimmy Macko another notch. The boy had some common sense to go along with his courage. "Sure." Luther hadn't owned a weapon smaller than .36 caliber in his life, but he figured he could spare some change to buy a hurt boy some reassurance.

"I got no money," Jimmy said apologetically. "I can't pay for them."

"Don't worry about it," Luther said. "A few cartridges are nothing between friends." He rose and reached for his hat. "You'd better get some rest, Jimmy. I'll leave the shells with Aunt Martha."

Alarm flared in the boy's eyes. "Aren't you coming back to see me?"

Luther almost shook his head, but the expression in the brown eyes stopped the motion. It had never dawned on Luther that the boy might be lonely—not with Martha Turlock around. "I'll be back, Jimmy. I'll bring you the ammunition this afternoon. For now, you need to rest. You can't do anything about those men until you're well again." He headed for the door.

"Travis?"

Luther turned. The boy's eyes were closed now. He was losing the battle against sleep and the release from pain it would bring. "Yes?"

"Thanks. For—for being my friend." The thin voice trailed away. Jimmy Macko's breathing deepened and became more regular. The boy was asleep.

Luther stood for a moment and stared down at the small form on the cot. He had thought he was beyond the reach of another person's emotions, that he had perfected the art of not letting any bonds or ties develop. He knew now that he had been wrong. Luther hated to admit it, but the boy's trust and friendship had touched him.

He strode from the room. Martha Turlock dozed in an armchair in the living room. She came awake with a start as Luther entered. "Is Jimmy all right?"

Luther smiled in reassurance. "He's fine, Mrs. Turlock. He's fallen asleep." He studied her bloodshot green eyes, the new wrinkles in her forehead. "It looks like you could use some more rest, too."

Martha rose to her feet. "I should be with him. In case he needs something. Maybe I can catch a nap in the chair by the bed while he's sleeping."

"Mrs. Turlock, thank you. For taking such good care of the boy."

Martha smiled back. "He got to you, too, didn't he?"

Luther sighed. "Yes, ma'am. I guess he did. I promised Jimmy I'd come back this afternoon—if that's all right with you. I don't want to tire the boy, but I'd sure like to see him one more time before I move on."

Martha Turlock placed a hand on Luther's muscular forearm. "I can't think of a single reason why not," she said. Her smile faded. "Jimmy needs a friend desperately now, Mr. Travis. The poor child's lost so much. . . ." Her voice trailed away in sympathy. She swallowed hard and forced a wan smile. "You come back about three o'clock. He should be awake again by then."

Luther watched as the marshal's wife walked toward the door. I'll bet she was a looker in her prime, Luther thought, and a good, gentle woman, too. There aren't many like her around.

He paused in the doorway and glanced both ways along the street from long habit. He saw no obvious threat. Luther stepped into the dusty thoroughfare, tugged his hat down against the growing wind, and strode toward the general store. As he walked, he noted potential ambush sites. The narrow spaces between buildings, shadowed alleyways, even the rooftops of adobe structures or the bell tower of the church could hold an enemy. In a town, there were fewer places of safety than there were on a lonely wilderness trail.

Three men were in front of the café. Marshal Turlock leaned on his cane beside the two full-time members of the local spit-and-whittle club, talking quietly with the old-timers on the bench. Turlock turned to study Luther as he passed on the far side of the street, but made no move to intercept him. Still, Luther could feel the old marshal's stare follow him into the general store.

The tall, paunchy man behind the counter looked up as Luther walked in. The shopkeeper's thin face bunched in a scowl. Luther could see at a glance that the man didn't like him. It was fair enough. The feeling was mutual.

"Something you need?" The shopkeeper's words were a challenge as much as a question.

"Couple of boxes of ammunition. One twenty-two, one forty-five Colt."

The store owner plucked two boxes from a shelf and plopped them down before Luther. "Fifteen cents for the twenty-twos, fifty cents for the big ones."

Luther frowned. The price was considerably higher than anywhere else on the frontier. But when a man had the only store for miles around, he could charge damn near whatever he wanted. Luther fished coins from his pocket, tossed sixty-five cents on the counter, and picked up the ammunition.

"You don't look like a man would carry a twenty-two," the shopkeeper said. "Camp gun?"

Luther locked a cold stare on the bridge of the thin nose. "That, mister, is none of your business."

The tall man tried to hold Luther's stare and failed. "Most anything that goes on in this town is my business," he grumbled.

"Asking a lot of fool questions is a good way to get that beak of a nose of yours tweaked," Luther said, his voice low and hard. "Besides, I charge five dollars an answer. Be sure you can afford it before you push."

Luther turned and strode from the store, the anger digging at his gut. Nosiest damn town I've ever been in, he thought. The warmth of aggravation began to cool as he headed down the street toward Amy Caldwell's boardinghouse. He was anxious to get back on the trail, but he wasn't inclined to ride out on Jimmy after he'd promised to visit the boy again. And come to think of it, he mused, the idea of spending a little more time with Amy Caldwell wasn't exactly repulsive.

Luther paused at the edge of the street to stare toward the hills along the river. His gaze lingered on the spot where he had found the ashes of the small camp fire and the moccasin footprints. He saw nothing. No sign of movement that couldn't be explained by the wind or the play of sunlight on rocks and stubby, twisted junipers. He wasn't reassured. He still had that itchy feeling in his gut that couldn't be scratched.

The tall man who lay beneath the overhanging branches of a thick juniper breathed a sigh of relief. The big man in the street below seemed to have been staring straight through him for a long time before he finally turned and went into the two-story house.

Hoss Duggan waited another few minutes, then squirmed from beneath the evergreen, crawling on his belly like a snake wriggling backward. Only when he was sure he was safely out of sight beyond the crest of the rocky hill did he rise to his feet. He slapped an oversized hand against the red ant that had been stinging the hell out of his left forearm and rubbed the fiery spot.

The ant sting didn't amount to much now, though it had taken every bit of Duggan's willpower not to take a swat at the critter. Not while the big man in the street stood and stared at the hill. The welt would burn like old billy blazes for a while. But the man in the street would be feeling something a lot hotter pretty soon. Duggan eased his way back to his horse, tethered to a dead tree halfway down the west side of the hill overlooking Cimarron. He lifted his canteen and took a few swallows, splashed a bit of water over the welt left by the ant, and squatted in the scant shade cast by the big roan gelding.

It shouldn't be that much of a problem, he told himself silently. He knew where the big man was. And now he knew where to wait for him. The narrow alley between the blacksmith shop and the empty harness store was almost straight across the street from the boardinghouse.

It would be an easy shot. That jasper was a dead man. He just hadn't fallen down yet.

Duggan rolled a cigarette and smoked as he finalized his ambush plans. He could ride a half-circle to the south, leave the roan on the far side of the ridge, Injun his way through the rocks and juniper and then through the mesquite thicket that ran almost to the back of the blacksmith's shop.

Duggan squinted through the smoke and nodded, satisfied with his plan. He had learned his trade well. Seven men had gone down in Duggan ambushes. Not a one of them had even seen his face. A couple of quick slugs between the shoulder blades and get out, that was Duggan's creed. It did away with the risk. No matter how good a man was with a gun, his talent faded fast with two soft lead .44 slugs in his back. Doing the job in a town complicated things some, but there was always a few seconds of confusion before anybody started to hunt the shooter. That was plenty of time.

He crushed the cigarette butt beneath the heel of a worn boot, slipped his .44 New American from the holster, and chambered a sixth round. Normally he carried five rounds in the cylinder, leaving the chamber under the hammer empty. He had never needed more than a couple of cartridges to do a job. But a man never knew, that one extra round might mean the difference.

Duggan dropped the .44 back into the holster and mounted the leggy gelding. He felt nothing toward the big man in the boardinghouse. It didn't matter a whit to Duggan that the man had killed Dolph Scarborough. Somebody would have, sooner or later. Dolph had always been dumb. Kept dealing himself into hands without checking to see who the other players were. Last time, he'd drawn a deuce instead of an ace.

Duggan's loyalties lay with gold coin. Tyler Scarborough wanted the big man dead bad enough to put a hundred dollars on his head. That was reason enough for Hoss Duggan. That and the woman who had stepped out onto the porch and spoken to the man. Even from a distance Duggan could tell she was some kind of looker, with a body to make any man paw the ground. In a few days, when Scarborough's boys owned Cimarron, Duggan would help himself to the blonde. The thought brought a smile. She looked like the kind who would fight. That always made it more fun. Hoss

Duggan liked it even more when they hurt bad enough to scream out loud.

He reined the roan toward the south and chuckled to himself. Hell, he thought, Tyler could have saved hisself some money. I'd have done it just for the woman.

Luther McCall sat at Jimmy's side, pleased with what he saw.

The boy had gotten a touch of color back into his cheeks. There was no sign of fever, and he seemed stronger than he had during the morning visit. Luther knew the boy still wasn't out of the woods. Anything could happen with a gunshot wound. But he was on his way.

The mid-afternoon sun baked the dusty street outside, but within the thick adobe walls of the Turlock home it was pleasant enough, almost cool.

"Thanks for the shells, Travis," Jimmy said. The cardboard box with a hundred rounds of .22 Short cartridges lay beside the Remington rifle.

Luther waved a hand. "No problem. How are you doing this afternoon?"

"It doesn't hurt quite as bad." Jimmy's voice sounded stronger, but Luther could hear the lingering weakness behind the words. "I just wish I could get out of this bed. There's nothing to do."

"Maybe I should have brought some cards or something," Luther said.

Jimmy's smooth brow furrowed in a quick frown. "I wish I had my books, Travis. They burned up when those men set fire to the house."

Luther raised an eyebrow. The boy was full of surprises. "You like books?"

Jimmy sighed. "Sure do. Pa didn't care much for me reading, though. Said if I had time to waste, he'd find some more chores for me. Uncle Ed argued with Pa some about that. Ed couldn't read a lick, but he figured it wasn't hurting anyone if I did."

"I agree with your Uncle Ed," Luther said. "Any books in particular you like to read?"

Jimmy carefully raised a hand and scratched behind his ear. "Not really. Just those with words on the pages and stories to tell. Sometimes Pa took my books away when he was mad at me. Then I'd read the labels on flour sacks and coffee cans."

Luther smiled. "Jimmy, you're sounding more like me every time I talk to you. I'll see what I can do. And if I can't find you some books of your own in this town, I bet I know someone who would be happy to read to you." Amy would jump at the chance, Luther knew. She could probably add a lot to Jimmy's education in the process.

"That sure would be nice, Travis. I don't get so bored when there's a book to read." Jimmy sighed. "Only book Aunt Martha has is an old Bible. It's not as much fun to read as real stories. There's too much begattin' in the Bible. Hard to keep track of who's who."

"I skip that part myself," Luther said, smiling. "I'll see what I can do. Anything else you need?"

Jimmy winced at a fresh twinge of pain, then forced a weak grin. "New shoulder would be nice."

"Now that," Luther said, "I can't help you with. You'll just have to take it slow, do what Aunt Martha says, and grow that one back together." He stood. "I'll be back in a few minutes."

The storekeeper glanced up from his ledger as Luther stepped into Holloway's Emporium. "What do you want now, mister?"

Luther's eyes narrowed. He didn't like the tone of the man's voice. He checked the sudden flare of temper. "I'm looking for some books."

"Books? What does a man like you need books for?"

Luther leaned forward and gripped the edge of the counter with his free hand. It was the only way he could keep himself from slamming a fist into the narrow nose. "What a man like me needs books for," he said, his voice like ice, "is none of your business. You got any books or not?"

The shopkeeper glared at Luther for a few heartbeats, then shrugged. "I dunno," he said. "Don't get much call for 'em out here. But I took a couple boxes of stuff on account when old man Carleton gave up his homestead and left a spell back. Seems I remember there might be a book in one of the boxes in the back storeroom. I'll check."

The storekeeper was gone for five minutes. He returned with a couple of dusty leather-bound volumes and tossed them onto the counter. "That's all there was," he said.

Luther picked up one of the books and blew the dust from the cover. It was a Dickens book, *A Tale of Two Cities*, dog-eared, its once stiff spine broken from frequent use. The other was Scott's *Ivanhoe*, equally worn and tattered. Luther briefly wondered if the two books might be too difficult for Jimmy. But they were books, and Amy could help if Jimmy got in over his head with them.

"I'll take them," he said.

"Fifty cents each."

Luther glared at the storekeeper. "For somebody who has no use for books, you're damn proud of them," he said.

The tall man shrugged. "That's the price. Take it or leave it."

Luther pulled a silver dollar from his pocket and slammed it onto the countertop. He felt a muscle in his jaw twitch as he stared into the lean face. Then he spun on a heel and strode out into the blast furnace of afternoon sun and wind.

Josh Turlock was waiting in the front room when Luther returned. The marshal sat in a chair facing the door, his cane leaning against the table. "About ready to move on?"

Luther gritted his teeth, trying to control his temper. The lingering aggravation with the shopkeeper wasn't helping his mood any. "We've whipped this horse before, Marshal. If you want to run me out of town, let's get on with it. Otherwise, I'll leave when I'm good and ready."

Turlock didn't flinch. "We'll talk about it later, Travis. Jimmy's waiting for you."

The boy's face brightened as Luther walked into the room, the two books under his arm. It seemed to Luther that a bit more color came to the pale, drawn cheeks. Luther held out the Dickens book. Jimmy almost dropped it; he was still too weak to heft even the slight weight of the book. It became obvious to Luther that the problem was only half solved.

With one bad shoulder, the youth couldn't hold the book up to read and turn the pages.

It took a half hour of trial and error—sometimes causing the boy pain, but he never whimpered—before they found the answer. Martha Turlock, checking to see that Luther wasn't taxing Jimmy's strength too much, provided the key. It was a metal brace used to hold her one treasure, a china plate with a painting of Christ on the surface. The bottom of the rack held the book open. With a careful positioning of pillows against the headboard she managed to prop Jimmy up to a sitting position, his knees raised, and placed the rack and book against his thighs. It would be slow going, Luther knew, but at least Jimmy could now read in bed while he recovered.

Satisfied, Luther reached for his hat. "If you have any trouble with the words or what Mr. Dickens meant when he wrote something, ask Mrs. Turlock or Amy Caldwell to help."

Jimmy glanced up. "Why can't I just ask you, Travis?"

The question was like a knife in Luther's gut. He hadn't yet come to terms with the idea of saying good-bye. He hadn't expected to get so attached to the boy. It was an almost forgotten feeling for Luther McCall; years had passed since he had felt the closeness of friendship and sharing and the pain of parting. He sighed. "I'll be moving on soon, Jimmy," he said softly.

For a moment, hurt that wasn't physical pain glistened in the boy's brown eyes. Then he swallowed and nodded. "I sort of expected that, I guess." He tried but failed to keep the note of disappointment from his voice.

Luther swallowed against the unfamiliar tightness in his throat. "Jimmy, it's not that I want to leave. It's that I have to go. Maybe someday you'll understand."

"Will you come back—to say good-bye?"

"I don't know, Jimmy. I don't believe in making promises I might not be able to keep. But I'll try." Luther turned and walked from the room. He wasn't good at this sort of thing.

The feeling of emptiness stayed in him as he made his way down the main street toward Amy Caldwell's boardinghouse. It was time to leave Cimarron.

CHAPTER
SIX

Luther McCall tugged the single-fire saddle cinch tight on the black and reached for the lead rope of Chili's halter. The brown was feeling antsy this afternoon. Luther was in no mood for a pitching contest, so he had saddled the more docile black. Chili stood on the black's off side now, ears laid back against the brown neck, the whites of his eyes showing. It was a look that told Luther that Chili had some outrage in mind.

He looked past the brown. Marshal Josh Turlock leaned against his cane a block away, staring toward Luther. The sight stirred a fresh ripple of irritation. Luther was getting more than a little tired of having a broken down old lawman for a shadow. It seemed that he couldn't go anywhere in Cimarron without having the old coot on his tail. Luther would miss Jimmy, and Amy Caldwell, but he sure as hell wasn't going to miss that man.

He dismissed the marshal's presence from his mind. In a few hours the old man with the cane would be a memory, left behind with the miles.

Luther glanced at Amy Caldwell, who stood on the low porch beside the door of the boardinghouse. He thought he saw a brief expression of regret in the gold-flecked, dark blue eyes. Luther felt a bit of a twinge himself. He liked Amy Caldwell. She was open, honest, educated—and sure as hell not hard to look at, either. That made her a dangerous combination for a man in Luther's position.

"Will you be coming back to Cimarron, Travis?"

Luther shook his head. "I doubt it, Amy. But again, I never know where the trail will lead. Keep an eye on Jimmy for me, will you?"

Amy smiled. The flash of teeth seemed even brighter in the pure white light of the afternoon sun. "I'll do so, with pleasure. I could write you and keep you updated on his progress if you like."

Luther winced. "I would like that very much, Amy, but I don't know where I might be a week from now, or a month or a year."

"It must be a lonely life," Amy said softly.

"Sometimes. But it suits me." Luther lifted his fingertips to his hat brim in a farewell salute. He toed the stirrup and reached for the horn to mount.

Chili picked just that instant to display his ill temper. The brown bared his teeth and snapped at the black's neck; the black twisted and lunged to escape the sudden attack. The black's shoulder thumped into Luther, staggered him a step—and saved his life.

Luther heard the distinct whop of lead against flesh a split second before the blast of the pistol shot rattled the air. He whirled and drew his Colt, the motion a blur of instinct. He cocked the weapon as it cleared leather and leveled the muzzle toward a tall, lanky shape in the shadows of the narrow alley across the street. He squeezed the trigger, and the handgun slammed against his palm. Through the blast of black powder smoke, he saw the tall figure sag and turn. Fire flashed from the alley. A second slug whirred past Luther's ear. Luther took his time, thumbed the hammer back, and stroked the trigger.

The man in the alley stumbled back, folded at the middle by the impact of the heavy slug. His pistol slipped from his fingers. He sank to his knees, an arm wrapped across his belly.

Luther cocked the Colt again, leveled the sights, and was about to drive a chunk of lead into the man's head when Amy Caldwell's gasp cut through the killing instinct that gripped him. He spun toward Amy.

She stood beside the doorway, a trickle of blood seeping down her arm. "Amy! Are you—" The sudden impact of a horse's shoulder against his side cut off Luther's call. Luther leapt aside as the black's knees buckled. The horse went down, hooves flailing at the dust of the street. Luther saw the pulse of crimson from the horse's neck. The bush-whacker's bullet had hit the black a handbreadth behind the throatlatch and severed an artery. Chili, spooked by the blood and gunfire, lunged against the lead rope, broke free, whirled, and ran down the street, hooves flinging dust.

Luther sprinted from the dying horse to Amy's side. "Are you hurt?" He asked her.

Amy stared for a moment at the blood on her arm, her eyes wide in shock and surprise. "I—don't think so. It didn't feel—like a bullet."

Luther heard the thump of Josh Turlock's cane as the old marshal hurried toward the shooting. He ignored the lawman's approach. He holstered the Colt, reached out and plucked at the material of Amy's housedress, then breathed a sigh of relief. A splinter torn from the door frame by the bullet that had passed near Luther's head had imbedded itself in the muscle of her upper arm just below the shoulder. The jagged end of the wood sliver protruded from the flesh.

"It doesn't look bad, Amy," Luther said. He heard the tight rage in his words as he eased her into a chair on the porch. "That damn fool could have killed you. Wait here."

Luther dodged past the dying black and sprinted toward the alley, the Colt back in his hand. He skidded to a stop six feet from the kneeling man, handgun leveled and ready. He saw at first glance he wouldn't be needing the next shot. A dark red stain spread over the man's belt buckle. Blood also flowed from a hole low on his rib cage. Both of Luther's slugs had found their marks.

He kicked the downed man's pistol out of reach, then lowered the Colt's hammer, but kept the weapon in his hand. The tall man raised his head, his face pale and twisted with pain. "You gut-shot me," he said in disbelief.

"That's what I had in mind. You nearly killed an innocent woman, you son of a bitch," Luther snapped. "I'd put a slug in your head except for one thing—I want to see you die slow and hard for that. Now, who are you and why did you try to bushwhack me?"

Luther heard the limping gait of Marshal Josh Turlock round the corner of the alleyway. He glanced up as Turlock stopped, breathing hard, an ancient Remington .44 cap and ball revolver in a weathered hand. Luther ignored him.

"You big . . . bastard," the wounded man gasped. "Hadn't been for . . . that damn horse . . . I'd have nailed you good."

"I don't like back shooters," Luther said through clenched teeth. He jabbed the barrel of the Colt into the man's bullet-torn belly. The tall man screamed in agony. "I know ways to make a man hurt real bad," Luther said, his tone icy. "Talk to me."

The wounded man gasped for breath and finally raised his head. His eyes were glazed with pain. "You may have killed me . . . but, by God, you're a dead man . . . too."

"I'm feeling a sight friskier than you are, mister, but I'm running out of patience." Luther jabbed him again with the Colt.

The man's breath whistled through his teeth.

"Hold up a minute, Travis," Josh Turlock said. "No use torturing a man who's going to die anyway." The marshal knelt stiffly by the wounded man's side and peered into the twisted face. "I know you. Hoss Duggan. You ride with Tyler Scarborough's gang."

A flicker of anger showed through the pain in Duggan's eyes. "Tyler's gonna kill you for this—and for Dolph." His breath came in quick, labored gasps. "And he's gonna take it out on this town. He's bringin' every man he's got. Few days from now Tyler'll own Cimarron."

Josh Turlock glanced at Luther, then stared back at the tall man. "Tell me about that, Duggan."

"Go . . . to hell, you . . . crippled up old bastard!"

Turlock sighed. "All right, Travis, go ahead. Give him another poke."

Luther did.

A few minutes later, they had the whole story. Tyler Scarborough and his gang were headed for Cimarron to turn the place into a stronghold for bandits. "I just want to live long enough to see you die, you big son of a bitch," Duggan concluded. A new blast of agony shuddered through the lean body. "For Christ's sake . . . get me . . . a doctor."

Luther slowly became aware that a crowd had gathered. The blacksmith, the lean storekeeper with the potbelly, a tall man in a top hat and swallow-tailed frock coat Luther had never seen before, and a couple of cowboys from the saloon. It seemed to Luther that the whole town of Cimarron had been drawn to the gunfire. A ripple of muted conversation made the rounds of onlookers.

Josh Turlock leaned on his cane and heaved himself to his feet. "George, you and Otis haul this man over to the cantina. Put him in the back room." The shopkeeper and the powerful blacksmith stepped forward, hoisted the wounded man none too gently, and carried him away. "The rest of you, get back to your business," Turlock said. "Show's over."

Luther casually flipped open the loading port of the Colt, worked the ejector rod to kick out the empty hulls, and thumbed fresh cartridges into the handgun.

"I'll be taking the pistol, Travis," the marshal said, his tone steady and firm.

Luther leveled a cold stare at the marshal. "No, you won't. You saw the whole thing, Marshal. This man tried to bushwhack me. He killed my best horse and almost killed Amy. Nobody takes my guns unless they kill me first. Think you're up to that chore?"

Josh Turlock didn't blink. "Maybe. Maybe not." Then he casually shrugged. "It was self-defense, sure enough. I guess you can keep your guns. But you're not leaving town until I can call an inquest."

Luther holstered the reloaded Colt and flashed a humorless smile. "Make up your mind, Marshal. You've been trying to run me out of town ever since I got here. Now you're telling me I've got to stay."

"Things have changed, Travis. I may not look like much of a lawman, but I still wear the badge in this town. And I don't like the way things are shaping up here. If Hoss Duggan was telling the truth, we're right at the edge of a war. And you're the man who brought it to us."

Luther shrugged. "That's no concern of mine, Marshal."

"Maybe it is, maybe it isn't. We'll see." Turlock nodded toward the boardinghouse. Martha Turlock was at Amy Caldwell's side, peering at the wound in the blond woman's arm muscle. The man in the frock coat came into view around the church, riding a long-eared buckskin horse and leading Luther's brown. "Meantime," Turlock said, "we've got a dead horse to drag off and a hurt woman to care for. Let's go."

An hour later the black mare's body was gone, sand raked over the immense pool of blood that had pumped from the horse's neck. Amy Caldwell sat in a chair by the table in the boardinghouse, a bandage bulked beneath the cloth of a clean housedress. Her face was pale, but she held her chin high.

"I'm sorry about your horse, Travis," she said.

"Don't fret about that, Amy. Horses can be replaced. You can't. It's my fault you almost got killed. That fellow was after me, not you."

Amy started to shrug, but winced as the wound in her arm reminded her that such moves weren't a good idea. She sighed. "No serious damage done. Don't blame yourself, Travis. What happens, happens."

Josh Turlock frowned. "That's true, Amy. What we have to worry about is what happens now." He told Amy and Martha what he and Luther had learned in the alley. The muscles in Amy's jaw tightened as the marshal finished his story.

"Marshal," Amy said firmly, "we can't let that bunch of outlaws take over Cimarron. It's our town, and we have too much of our lives invested in it. What do you plan to do?"

The marshal's brow furrowed. "We've got to have a town meeting, like we always do when a problem comes along. I'll call it for tonight, in the church. We'll decide then what would be best." Turlock sighed. "I don't want to see this town treed by a bunch of outlaws any more than you do, Amy. But I don't want to see any of our people dead, either. It's going to be a tough call." The marshal turned to glare at Luther. "You're going to be there too, Travis."

Luther returned the marshal's stare. "It's not my affair, Turlock."

"That wasn't a social invitation. You'll be there."

Luther stared hard into the leathery face. He had no trouble reading the expression in the old man's hazel eyes.

Josh Turlock had seen Luther's speed with a gun. And he wasn't the least damn bit worried.

Josh Turlock stood behind the pulpit in the small white-washed church. Luther McCall sat off to one side, alone on a hard wooden pew.

Luther's gaze drifted over the crowd. It looked to him like every person in Cimarron was there. Word of the shooting and impending raid had spread like wildfire soon after the echoes of the shots had died away.

Luther knew several faces in the crowd. George Winfield, the blacksmith, sat scowling in a front row pew. Martha Turlock, her gray hair pulled into a tight bun and worry wrinkles creasing her forehead, sat beside Winfield. To her left Amy Caldwell waited patiently, her expression calm, the bulge at her shoulder hinting at the bandage beneath. If she felt pain, Luther noted, she didn't show it.

Otis Holloway, the storekeeper with the thin frame and potbelly, sat behind Martha. His face was pale, and his Adam's apple bobbed almost constantly in the scrawny neck. The two old-timers who made up Cimarron's spit-and-whittle club sat apart from the others. From time to time one or both glanced suspiciously at Luther. He ignored their sideways glances.

The man in the frock coat who had retrieved Luther's panicked brown horse after the shooting was there, his expression outwardly serene. The wiry, silver-haired, former cowboy who ran the cantina sat with his arms folded, bushy eyebrows lifted in anticipation of the debate that was about to begin. The two cowpunchers who frequented the cantina sat beside the bartender. Three men and two women who bore the tired, worn-down look of homesteaders—farmers, most likely—slumped in a rear pew. Luther had never seen them before. Probably folks who lived outside town on a hardscrabble outfit that never would pay the bills, he figured. Neil Braden, the café owner Luther had come to know slightly, sat in a pew near the back, heavy arms crossed over his ample belly, the legacy of sampling too many specialties from his own kitchen. There was no expression in the close-set, puffy eyes. Luther knew a few of the others by sight; a half dozen or so were strangers to him.

Luther was the only one in the group who carried a sidearm. It was the custom in Cimarron to leave all weapons in the foyer before entering the sanctuary. Luther defied the tradition. He made it a point never to be more than arm's length away from his weapons. Besides, in Luther's mind a church wasn't all that holy a place. The Creator's work was outside, in the vast expanse of prairie and towering mountains, under a sky that was bright blue or boiling with storm clouds, where antelope and deer and an occasional buffalo watched cautiously as a man rode past. Church buildings got in the way of religion. Luther had never needed anyone to act as a go-between. He spoke to the Creator directly when the urge struck. That wasn't often. Luther was not a particularly religious man, but he sensed that something or someone was behind the existence of this place called Earth. And, he mused, at the core he was more Indian than Christian when it came to the concept of creation and spirits. The Indians had a better working relationship with the Great Spirit, by whichever name they called Him. There was no hypocrisy in their prayers and ceremonies. Indians were sincere with their religions. A man couldn't always say that about the whites.

Marshal Josh Turlock interrupted Luther's musings. He cleared his throat and stood for a moment, looking over the audience. The low murmurs of muted conversations faded expectantly. All eyes turned toward the old man with the cane behind the pulpit.

"I suppose you all know why we're here," Turlock said. His voice was calm, confident, and carried well throughout the small chapel. "The Scarborough gang is coming to take over our town. We've got to decide—and quick—what to do about that. The man who was shot in the gunfight said we had just a few days before Scarborough and his bunch get here." He paused for a moment to let the urgency of the message sink in. "I've called this town meeting for the same reason we've had them in the past. Everyone has a say in what happens in Cimarron, and every man or woman here will be heard. I'm opening the floor for discussion."

Otis Holloway stood and jabbed a long, bony finger toward Luther. The finger trembled. "It's this man's fault we're in this mess," Holloway said. "He killed Tyler Scarborough's brother, and now one of his men. He's the one to blame for bringing those gunmen down on our heads!"

A few voices muttered in agreement and several heads nodded.

"I say," Holloway all but shouted, "we just hand this drifter over to Scarborough. Then they'll go away and leave us alone."

Two of the homesteaders nodded in agreement; most of the others in the crowd looked skeptical. All were staring at Luther, their expressions ranging from anger to curiosity to contempt. The looks started the anger glowing again in Luther's gut.

"We can't fight Scarborough," Holloway said. "Look at us—there's not a half dozen people here who can handle a gun. Scarborough's got a bunch of killers and gun hands with him. We'll all be dead if we go up against them. I say we give them the man they want."

One of the old-timers stood, ran weathered fingers through a beard stained with tobacco juice, and stared hard at Luther. "What you got to say about it, mister?" The question was an obvious challenge.

Luther shrugged. "It's none of my business," he said, his tone flat and calm. "Cimarron isn't my town." He shrugged. "I was on my way out when this happened. I still plan to ride on." He leveled a cold, hard stare at Otis Holloway. "If you people want to turn your bellies up and quit, that's your problem. Not mine."

An angry mutter swept through the gathering. "By God," one of the homesteaders said, "maybe Otis is right. Maybe we ought to just hang this man and hand the body over to Scarborough. Then they'd leave us alone."

Josh Turlock pounded a fist against the pulpit until the mutters stopped. He stood for a moment and stared at the faces in the crowd. "You people stop and think for a minute," he said. "Maybe this man did bring these outlaws down on us. Maybe he didn't—maybe they would have come anyway.

But there'll be no lynching bees in this town as long as I wear this badge."

Holloway snorted in disgust. "Turlock, everybody in this room knows the only reason you got that badge in the first place is because you fought for the Confederacy. We felt sorry for an old crippled soldier, that's all. Never thought we'd need a real lawman."

Josh Turlock's eyes narrowed. Otis Holloway blinked before the marshal's cold stare. "You're absolutely right, Otis," he said calmly. "I knew that from the day you folks handed me this badge. I owe this town. And, by God, it's time I paid you people back. Scarborough's bunch will get this town by riding over my dead body. No other way."

Luther grudgingly raised his opinion of the old marshal another notch. Josh Turlock had grit. He would fight. And he'd get killed. That was the pity of the whole thing.

"Maybe you folks haven't thought this through, either," Turlock said. "Scarborough wants more than this man Travis. He wants his own Hole in the Wall, his own Robber's Roost. And we've got it. Cimarron will be the biggest outlaw hangout north of Mexico if we let him take over."

"Dammit, Josh," Holloway said, "we can't fight professional gunmen—"

"We can try." George Winfield's booming voice cut through the storekeeper's comment. He rose to his feet, his face flushed in anger. "Holloway, who stands to gain the most if this town turns into an outlaw stronghold? Seems to me you'd make more money off Scarborough's gang than you do off the handful of poor folks we've got here."

Holloway sputtered in indignation, but Luther could see that the blacksmith's words had hit home. The shopkeeper would prosper with free-flowing cash from stolen horses, cattle, and other robberies. Luther had seen it happen more than once. A nice, quiet town wrecked because of the merchants' greed. The suspicious glances the crowd turned on Holloway told Luther they sensed the truth in George Winfield's words.

"I don't know about the rest of you people," Winfield said, "but I'm with Josh. I'll fight. We've got women to protect, too. Scarborough's men aren't going to stop at just taking the town." He paused for a moment to let that message sink in. "Now, folks, I made a lot of mistakes when I was a kid. I spent most of my life looking for a home. Now, I've found one. Nobody's going to take it away from me without a scrap."

Another murmur swept the crowd. But this time the tone was different, Luther noted; it wasn't anger directed at him. For the first time he became aware that Cimarron might have more backbone than he'd given the town credit for. And it was going to get them all dead. This bunch couldn't whip a ten-year-old Kiowa with a clubfoot, he thought, let alone professional gunmen. Scarborough's gang would go through them like Sherman went through Georgia.

Luther became aware of the sudden silence in the crowd. Amy Caldwell stood, her shoulders square, jaw set in defiance. "Gentlemen, I may only be a woman. But it doesn't take much physical strength to pull a trigger, and I know how to use a shotgun." A murmur of shock and surprise rose from the gathering. "Mr. Winfield is correct. This is our town, and it's up to us to keep it that way."

Martha Turlock rose and stood silently beside Amy. The two cowboys also came to their feet, the faint jingle of spur rowels loud in the sudden silence.

The shopkeeper and the homesteaders remained seated. The farmers glanced about nervously, fear etched in their lined faces. Finally, the tall man in the frock coat rose from his pew across the room.

"Ladies and gentlemen," he said, deep voice booming over the crowd, "I have been your lay preacher here for more than two years. It says in the Good Book that thou shalt not kill. That the meek will inherit the earth."

"Amen, Brother Alesworth," one of the farmers shouted.

The call brought only a cold stare from the lanky preacher. Alesworth strode to the front of the chapel and turned to glare at the crowd. "The Bible also says that the tribes rose up and smote the Philistines. The Bible calls upon man to be not overcome by evil, but to overcome evil with good. If the taking of a human life is evil, let us follow the Word of the

Book of Romans: 'Let us do evil, that good may come.' " He paused for a moment, then turned to Luther. "You, friend, have brought this pestilence down upon us. Now I beseech you to rectify that wrong. Again quoting the Good Book: 'Come over into Macedonia, and help us.' "

Luther was about to shake his head when Amy Caldwell's blue eyes caught his gaze. "Mr. Travis, we *do* need you," she said. "Most of us here are merchants, tradesmen, farmers. We are not warriors. But you know the ways of the gun. We need that talent to save our lives, our homes—and our town."

"No!" Holloway's yelp almost rattled the one small stained glass window behind the pulpit. The storekeeper was trembling in anger and fear. "It's his fault we're in this mess! I still say the only thing we can do is hand him over to that gang! Somebody get a rope!"

Luther's resolve to keep his mouth shut wilted under a fresh flare of rage and disgust. He stood, his narrowed eyes directing a steely, cold glare at Holloway. An expectant silence fell over the gathering. Luther waited for several heartbeats until he had checked the urge to drive a fist into the storekeeper's craggy face. "Why don't you just go get that rope yourself, Holloway?" His voice was calm, the tone icy, and it carried well in the small chapel.

Holloway swallowed several times, tried to hold Luther's stare and failed. He glanced at the homesteaders, hoping for support, and found none.

"This isn't my town, Holloway, and it isn't my fight," Luther said. "I'm riding out. Now. I don't intend to get myself shot on behalf of a coward like you. You can go straight to hell for all I care. Now go get that rope—or sit down and shut your mouth." Luther knew his stubbled cheeks were dark with rage, and he didn't care.

The creak of hinges at the church door broke the brief, tense silence. Luther crouched and whirled instinctively toward the door, hand dropping to the grip of the Colt at his hip, then froze and stared in surprise at the small figure outlined in the open frame.

Jimmy Macko stood in the doorway, wavering on his feet, the barrel of the old Remington .22 rifle gripped in a small, white-knuckled hand, the stock trailing on the floor behind him. A blood spot the size of a silver dollar showed crimson on the fresh white bandage across his shoulder. Then Jimmy's knees began to buckle, and he sagged against the doorway.

Luther sprinted to the boy's side and slipped a hand around his waist, stopping his fall. "Jimmy, what are you doing out of bed?"

Pain glazed the brown eyes, but the fire in them was not from fever. "I heard . . . about the meeting. I come to . . . to help fight." Jimmy's voice was faint, the weight of the frail, damaged body almost negligible in Luther's hand. "Those men . . . killed Pa . . . and . . . Uncle Ed. I got to pay them back, Travis. I got to. You ought to . . . know that . . . better'n anybody here." The Remington started to slip from Jimmy's fingers. Luther reached out and caught the weapon. The boy's eyes closed, and his muscles abruptly went slack.

Martha Turlock and Amy Caldwell reached Luther and the boy a few seconds later, the first in a surge of adults toward the door. Luther turned Jimmy over to the clucking voice and gentle hands of Martha Turlock, then stood erect. "The rest of you back off," Luther growled. "Give the boy some air." His gaze swept the crowd and settled on Otis Holloway's narrow face. "If you had a quarter of the backbone Jimmy Macko's got, Holloway, you'd be almost twice the man you are now."

The shopkeeper bristled, his face scarlet in anger and embarrassment. He blustered, his mouth working, but no words came out. He abruptly strode past Luther into the street outside the church.

Luther knelt beside the boy now cradled in Martha's broad lap. Jimmy was unconscious. Luther shook his head in silent wonder. The pain and the effort of walking the few steps from the Turlock home to the church must have been horrendous, he thought; not many grown men would have had the guts and determination to do that. "Is he going to be all right, Mrs. Turlock?"

Martha stripped away the thin shirt and peered at the bleeding shoulder. "This didn't help him any, Mr. Travis," she said without looking up, "but I'll have the bleeding stopped in a minute. He's still so weak. . . ." Her voice trailed away as she busied herself with the boy's wound.

Amy Caldwell, kneeling at Jimmy's side, lifted her gaze to Luther's face. "They'll kill him if we don't stop them," she said, her voice little more than a whisper. Luther knew her words were intended for him and him alone. "They'll find out he's here. That he can identify the men who killed his father and uncle. And they'll shoot him down like a stray dog." The deep blue eyes held a silent plea. "We can't stop Scarborough's gang without your help, Travis. You saved Jimmy once. Please don't let him die this time."

Luther stared down at the small, frail form in Martha's lap. His resolve to ride out, to leave Cimarron to a fate that didn't concern him, had taken a beating in a few words from a twelve-year-old boy and the pleading eyes of a blond woman. Dammit, Luther McCall, he groused to himself, why did you let these people get under your hide?

A touch on his shoulder interrupted his inner turmoil. Josh Turlock stood beside him. Luther, his concentration on the boy, hadn't heard the thump of the old lawman's cane. "I'd like a word with you outside, Travis. In private." The marshal's voice was firm but soft. Turlock scanned the faces gathered around the church door. "Those of you willing to fight, go with George over there. Tell him what weapons you have and how much ammunition. George, check with me in a couple of hours. We'll start working out a plan for defense."

Turlock's jawline seemed to tighten in anger as he stared at certain faces in the crowd. "The rest of you go home. If you won't help, then by God, stay out of the way." He turned to Luther and motioned toward the door with his chin. Turlock plucked his pistol belt from a peg as they went through the door and paused by the rusted cannon beside the church to strap the weapon on.

"Amy Caldwell's right, Travis," the marshal said as he buckled the belt into place and settled the holster on his hip. "That bunch will kill Jimmy sure as sin if they're not stopped. And that's not the whole story. Give me fifteen minutes. Then you can decide if you want to stay or ride."

Luther followed without speaking as Josh Turlock led the way to his office, a two-room adobe beside his house. The front room held a double-barreled shotgun in a rack beside the door, a battered desk cluttered with papers, two chairs, a potbellied stove with a coffeepot, and little else. The door to the back room stood open. Luther saw the cast-iron bars over the window, the heavy iron bar and big padlock lying on a three-legged stool beside the door. At least Cimarron had a lockup of sorts, Luther thought. He wondered if it had ever been used.

Turlock limped to the desk, eased himself with a grunt into the rickety chair behind it, and nodded for Luther to sit across from him.

"I'll lay it out for you short and simple, Travis," the marshal said. "First off, the man you shot in the alley died an hour ago. I went back through some old wanted flyers"—Turlock lifted an eyebrow at Travis—"and found out there was a hundred dollar reward out for Hoss Duggan. Wanted for murder in Missouri. Help us out here, and I'll verify the reward is yours."

Luther leaned back in the cane-bottomed chair. A hundred dollars was a lot of money. "And if I don't?"

"I never saw Duggan's body. Before you decide, let me finish." The old man stroked his bushy handlebar mustache. "Otis Holloway was wrong about a lot of things, but he was telling it straight about me and this badge. I lost half a leg at Shiloh. The people in this town gave me a marshal's badge and a few dollars a month because of that, not because I'm a lawman. It was a pension of sorts. Pity money, you might call it." A hard light flickered in the aging eyes. "I haven't fired a gun at a man since the war, Travis. I'm no fast gun. Just an old man with an antique pistol. But I'll tell you this—that bunch is going to have to go through me before they take my town. For once, I'm going to earn my pay."

Luther sighed. "That would be suicide, Marshal."

Turlock shrugged. "Everybody dies. It doesn't bother me that much to think about it anymore. Scarborough's bunch might tree Cimarron. But maybe, by God, they won't." He shifted his weight in the chair to ease the discomfort in his twisted leg. "Travis, you're a gun hand. You've been on the far side of the law. You understand how people like Tyler Scarborough think. I'm enough of a realist to know when I'm in over my head. That's one reason I'm asking for your help."

"Marshal," Luther said, "I don't—"

Turlock raised a hand. "Hear me out. Now, if Scarborough isn't stopped, he'll kill Jimmy. I know you're fond of the boy. God only knows what they'll do to Amy. Study on that for a minute. And chew on this, too—there are five men in Scarborough's outfit who have prices on their heads. Amounts to better than eight hundred dollars, counting Duggan."

Luther held back an urge to whistle. It was more money than he'd seen at one time since a high-stakes poker game in Deadwood during the gold rush days. "Are you offering me a split if we take them?"

The old marshal shook his head. "No. I'm saying you can have the whole damn poke. All I want is my town safe."

"It could be one of the toughest paydays a man ever worked for. Could be his last one, in fact."

Josh Turlock pulled a pipe from his pocket. "Could be. Nothing comes easy these days." He stuffed the pipe, scratched a match on the desk top and fired the tobacco, then squinted through the haze at Travis. "There's one more thing. Then I'll let you make up your own mind." He shook the match out just before the flame reached his fingers. "I found something else mighty interesting in that stack of old wanted notices."

Luther tensed. He had a good idea what the marshal had found. He waited silently, his face without expression.

"There's one of those fliers I could tear up. Sort of a bonus, you might say."

"And if I still say no?"

Turlock dragged at the pipe. He leveled a steady gaze at Luther, unblinking, unafraid. "Part of my job is to share information with other lawmen. The flier gets updated. That probably doesn't worry a man like you too much, Travis. But you might stir it into the stew I've served up here this afternoon. Chew on it a little. I've had my say. It's up to you now."

Luther propped his forearms against his knees and leaned forward. "I don't have to chew on it much, Marshal. I'll stay, and I'll help. But I want this much understood, up front—it's not because of any threat about a wanted flier. Or even reward money."

Turlock nodded. "Didn't figure it would be."

"I've seen something in this town, and in you, that I don't run across all that much," Luther said. "There's a few folks in Cimarron willing to fight for what they believe in. A youngster carrying a twenty-two rifle when he's too weak to walk. A couple of women who may have more guts than the rest of the town put together. And a stubborn old soldier who'll probably get us both killed." He sighed. "What the hell. Like you say, nobody lives forever. I'm in."

Josh Turlock nodded. "I have to tell you I'm damned glad you decided to stick around, Travis. Now, let's get some planning done."

CHAPTER
SEVEN

Tyler Scarborough's strides were quick and choppy, his boots kicking puffs of dust from sun-browned buffalo grass as he paced the campgrounds north of Raton. He paused from time to time to stare toward the northeast. Hoss Duggan was overdue. It wasn't like the lanky pistolero to be late. That raised a question, and Tyler Scarborough didn't like questions.

The Apache, Moondog, squatted by the small fire and dragged at a cigarette, his expression impassive as he watched Scarborough's nervous pacing. Carlos Vasquez sat with his back against a saddle and sipped at the neck of a quart of pulque. His one good eye watered at the fiery sting of the liquor in his gullet.

"Dammit," Scarborough growled aloud, "where is that long-legged son of a bitch? He was supposed to be back here last night."

Moondog took a final drag from his smoke and tossed the cigarette butt into the smoldering embers of the camp fire. "Won't be back," he said, his tone flat and as barren of expression as his black eyes.

Scarborough stared for a moment at the Apache. "What the hell you talkin' about?"

"Saw the Moon Wolf last night," Moondog said calmly. "It was carrying Duggan's head in its jaws."

Scarborough snorted in open contempt. "I thought I told you to leave that damn peyote alone until this job's done. Last thing we need is a superstitious Apache with his head in a whirlwind."

"Wasn't chewing peyote," Moondog said. "The Moon

Wolf came anyway. Duggan's dead. Might as well forget him."

Carlos Vasquez wiped the moisture from his eye and
stared at Moondog. The Apache was spooky. He saw things
no white man ever saw. Scarborough might think it was
just superstition, but Vasquez was more of a believer in
Moondog's medicine visions than any other man in the
band. If he said Duggan was dead, Duggan was dead.
Moondog's wolf was as real to Vasquez as the rosary he
carried in his vest pocket.

"Horse coming," Moondog announced. "Moving fast."

A full two minutes passed before the sound of hoofbeats
reached Vasquez's ears. How the hell does he do that?
Vasquez wondered. It's like he sees things before they
happen. Vasquez picked up his Winchester and levered a
round into the chamber.

"Relax, Carlos," Scarborough said with a frown. "It's
just Bates." Dark eyes narrowed in Scarborough's lined
face. "He damn well better have a good reason for riding
up on my camp like this."

La Cueva Sheriff Ned Bates reined his sorrel to a stop at
the edge of the outlaw camp. "You got problems, Tyler,"
the sheriff said. "Hoss Duggan's dead."

Scarborough cast a quick glance at Moondog, then shifted
his gaze to the sheriff. "What happened?"

"One of the nesters out by Cimarron rode in a little bit ago.
Damn near killed his horse getting here. Said the big man
who shot Dolph gunned down Duggan. Gut-shot him."

Scarborough barked a curse. "How in hell could this jasper
put lead in Duggan? Hoss never gave anybody a chance to
fight."

Bates swung down from the sorrel and wiped a hand
across the sweat that trickled from beneath his hatband.
"Duggan missed. It was his last mistake. That big man's
pure poison with a handgun, Tyler," he said, a touch of
awe in his voice. "But that ain't the worst of it. Duggan ran
off at the mouth some before he died. People in Cimarron
know you're coming."

Scarborough stared at the lawman for several moments,

rage and disgust flickering in his black eyes. "That complicates things some. Takes the element of surprise away from us." Then he sighed and shrugged. "Probably won't make any difference. That town'll turn belly-up when we ride in. They won't dare put up a scrap."

Bates fidgeted nervously with his hat brim. "They might, Tyler. That gun hand's going to help them. And that isn't the only bad news."

Scarborough snorted in disgust. "Damn if you're not just full of sunshine and happy yarns today, Bates. What the hell else?"

"The kid's there. In Cimarron."

Tyler's face twisted in a frown. "What kid?"

"The one Dolph thought they'd killed in the raid on the homestead. Turns out he isn't dead after all, just shot up some. The big man brought him into Cimarron."

Two of the riders who had gathered around the camp fire exchanged worried glances. They had ridden with Dolph on the raid. Having a witness around could land each of their necks in a noose.

Scarborough shrugged. "We'll take care of the kid after we tree Cimarron. No problem there." The black eyes narrowed in a squint. "The man who shot Dolph and Hoss is still in town, then?"

"Yeah."

"Good." Scarborough's thin lips twisted in a sneer. "I was afraid he'd light a shuck out of the country. I want that bastard. I'm going to butcher him like a fat steer and feed the pieces to the buzzards."

Ned Bates swallowed nervously. "Taking Cimarron may not be all that easy now, Tyler. That old marshal's got guts, and now he's got a top gun with him. The homesteader said the big man—calls himself Travis, by the way—sided with the townsfolk. Between the two of them, they could be trouble."

Tyler Scarborough's hand fell to the butt of the .41 Lightning at his hip. "Hell," he snorted in derision, "we got almost a dozen men and more on the way. Two can't stop us. We'll jump on Cimarron like a rooster on a grasshopper."

Bates again wiped a hand across his forehead. "There's more to it than that, Tyler. This homesteader says the marshal's got nearly the whole town on his side."

Scarborough spat in disgust. "Bates, you always were some kind of old woman when it came to shooting. A couple rifle slugs will take care of both problems, the marshal and this Travis fellow. The rest of the town won't fight, not when their stud ducks are dead and they see what they're up against."

Ned Bates squatted on his heels and reached for his tobacco sack. His fingers trembled, scattering tobacco flakes, as he rolled the smoke. "There might be an easier way, Tyler."

"You got something in your craw, Bates, spit it out."

Bates scratched a match and fired the quirly. "This settler says not everybody in town's wanting a fight. Fella named Otis Holloway—he owns the only general store there—sent a message with the clodhopper. He wants to make a deal."

"So what's he offering?"

"He'll give you this Travis fellow. And the kid. He'll make sure the old marshal doesn't get in the way. In return, you cut him in as a partner once you've got the town." Bates paused for a drag on the cigarette and let smoke trickle from his nostrils. "He could be a valuable man, Tyler. He's got connections with merchants and freighters from Tascosa to the Mexico border. Won't be a payroll, gold shipment, or trail drive moving that he won't know about."

Scarborough stared into the distance for a moment, then nodded. "All right, Bates. If this Holloway comes through with his end, we'll cut him in." He paused to jab a finger at the sheriff. "But you tell him that, by God, if he doesn't produce this Travis and the kid, I'll nail his corpse to the outside of his store. And I want the gunslinger alive."

Bates tossed his cigarette aside and mounted. "I'll get word to him. How much time you going to give him?"

Tyler Scarborough glanced over his shoulder toward nearby Raton. "I'm going to put some ground between me and Pat Garrett," he said. "I don't trust that long-legged son of a bitch to stop at the state line where his jurisdiction ends. We'll be moving out in a couple of hours." He patted the Colt again. "We'll be at Horse Springs on the Cimarron by sundown. I'll give this Holloway three days, starting tomorrow. Then we're coming in, one way or the other."

Scarborough stood silently and watched as Bates mounted and reined his horse back toward Raton. Carlos Vasquez waited until the sheriff had ridden from sight beyond a distant rise, then turned to Scarborough.

"Think this flour peddler can pull it off, boss?"

Scarborough shrugged. "Worth a try. We've got nothing to lose."

"And if he does? You really going to cut him in?"

Tyler Scarborough chuckled aloud. "Hell, no, Carlos. We'll kill the stupid bastard."

Otis Holloway stood in the darkened interior of his store and peered through the window toward the marshal's office at the end of the street. A light was still burning. He had watched Josh Turlock and the man called Travis go into the office a good two hours ago. If it was a war parley, he figured, it was a damn long one.

Despite the relative cool of the evening, Holloway felt sweat trickle down his back. His fingers trembled and his gut gurgled as he stared at the square patch of weak yellow lantern light. With every passing hour, his gut rumbled worse. He mentally cursed the whiskey-induced bravado that caused him to send old man Lansdale to Bates with his brash plan. Lansdale had ridden back in early this afternoon on a lathered horse with the news that Scarborough had bought the deal.

Now, Holloway was in a box. It would have been tough enough just to bushwhack this Travis with a scattergun; the man seemed to be looking everywhere at once, and he knew how to keep from being an open target. Now Scarborough had complicated the hell out of things. He wanted Travis and the kid alive. And if Holloway didn't produce them, Scarborough would nail him between the eyes with a lead slug.

The cramps hit Holloway's gut again. He hadn't been this scared in his life, even when that renegade Comanche bunch had hit the trading post back on the Wichita fifteen years ago. He had messed in his pants that time.

But there just might be a way.

The first and last thing Travis did every day was to visit Jimmy Macko. It was the only thing he did that came close to resembling a routine. It didn't make sense; men like Travis didn't care a whit for other people, but he had taken a shine to the wounded boy. Get to the kid first, Holloway thought, and use him to pull this Travis's teeth. A plan began to take shape in Holloway's mind. It still didn't help his churning guts all that much.

Luther McCall leaned forward to study the rough sketch of the town of Cimarron one final time, then grunted in satisfaction. He glanced at Josh Turlock's determined face and nodded.

"Only way they're likely to come at us is along the west bank of the river," Luther said. "Bluffs are too steep north and south, and it would take them several days to ride around town to attack from the east. I don't think Tyler Scarborough's got that much patience."

Turlock stroked a hand over his handlebar mustache. For the first time Luther noted the enlarged knuckles of the weathered hand, the stiffness of the fingers. Josh Turlock had more than a bad leg. Arthritis was slowly twisting his fingers. Within a few years he probably wouldn't even be able to hold a gun. If he lived that long.

"Seems logical," the marshal said, his voice calm and confident. "We've got a good field of fire if they come that way. Decent fortifications. We might be able to sucker them into a cross fire."

"Won't be too much of a cross fire," Luther said wryly. "We've got two cowboys, a blacksmith, a barkeep, a preacher, and a couple others besides you and me. That's nine people, and not many of them have ever shot at somebody who's shooting back. I'm not sure how many of them will actually fight when the guns start going off. We're up against a dozen or more hard cases, every one of them shooters. If I was asked to lay a bet on this one, Marshal, I'd bet against us."

Turlock reached for his pipe. "Maybe it is a lost cause, and maybe not. Don't underestimate the people of Cimarron,

Travis. They've got a lot to lose."

"Including their lives."

The marshal ignored Luther's comment. He touched the well-chewed stem of the pipe to several penciled squares representing buildings. "Put a rifleman here. Another here, a couple of people with shotguns here. Those two cowboys on rooftops here, and here. They look like they know how to handle a long gun."

"What about you, Marshal?"

Turlock raised cold hazel eyes to Luther. "I'm going to be standing in the middle of the square, Travis. Right beside the town well. Somebody's got to pull them into an ambush. I'm the bait."

"That will most likely get you killed."

"Maybe. I never got past the rank of private, but I still learned that in a military campaign you sometimes have to sacrifice a squad to save a battalion, and this is nothing if not a military operation." Turlock straightened in his chair and shrugged his shoulders. Luther saw no regret, no fear, in the old man's deeply lined face, only a stoic determination.

"Turlock," Luther said, "you and I both know they'll cut you to pieces out there. You said yourself you're no gunman."

The marshal sighed. "True enough. I'm not even sure these old eyes can still pick up the sights. But for once, I'm going to earn my pay." Turlock limped to the window and stared for a moment into the darkness. "I never had a place to call home before, Travis. Cimarron may not be much now, but it will be someday. In a few years we'll be a state, not a territory. We'll have courts and real law enforcement officers. Cimarron's in the right place to grow when that happens. We've got good water, a river crossing, and the hills break the winter winds. And for the most part we have good, upstanding, God-fearing people." The old man turned from the window to stare at Luther. "No outlaw gang is going to take my town, Travis."

Luther heard the quiet determination in the old man's tone. Even if nobody else believes Josh Turlock, Luther mused, Turlock believes himself. He may get killed, but he'll take some renegades with him. Luther pushed back his chair and stood. "One thing we need to know, Marshal," he said, "is when Scarborough's bunch is coming. Tomorrow I'll saddle up and do some scouting around."

Turlock turned back toward the window. "It's a big country out there, Travis. You can't cover it all yourself. I don't ride as much as I used to on account of this damn leg, but I can still fork a horse for a few hours at a stretch. I'll saddle up three hours before daylight and make a swing along the south bank. That's where the best camps are, the best water."

Luther picked up his Winchester and reached for the door latch. "I'll go along."

Turlock waved off the suggestion. "It's better if one of us stays in town. We need one leader here in case Scarborough comes. These people will need someone to tell them what to do. They don't have the experience to handle Scarborough alone. I'll be back around noon tomorrow. If I don't find anything, you ride out the country on the north side of the river."

"Makes sense."

"There's another reason I don't want us both out of town at the same time, Travis," Turlock said. "It's a selfish reason. I want someone watching out for Jimmy and Martha." The expression in the hazel eyes softened. "Martha and I have done a lot of talking in the past few days. Jimmy's got no family left. The boy's alone in the world now, and that's not healthy for a youngster. We've gotten attached to that boy. We're getting a little long in the tooth to raise another family—our only son's been buried in the Cimarron cemetery for nearly twenty years—but we're going to adopt Jimmy as our own when this mess is over."

Luther swung the door open. "I'm glad to hear that, Marshal. The boy will be in good hands. I'll check in on them first thing in the morning."

Luther stepped into the street, his gut swirling in a mixture of worry and relief. Jimmy would have a home, a home like Luther had had so briefly and then lost. If they all lived past the next few days. He paused for a breath of the night air. The heat faded fast when the sun went down in the Cimarron Strip, and the wind died along with the sunshine.

The air was almost cool now, the scent of dust yielding to the aroma of wood smoke that lingered from cooking fires. The only sounds along the street were muted and lazy as Cimarron settled in for the night. A horse neighed in the distance, a pup yipped at some shadow, and an owl prowled the outskirts of town on silent wings.

Luther had the unsettling feeling that he could close his eyes and be back in the Nebraska town of his own youth. It was unsettling because, for the first time in years, he actually gave a damn about someone besides himself and the men he sometimes hunted. Dammit, Luther, he scolded himself silently, you're breaking McCall's First Law of Survival: Never get involved in other people's lives. It may wind up killing you.

He sighed, shifted the Winchester to his left hand, and strode toward Amy Caldwell's boardinghouse near the end of the street. At least tomorrow he would be doing something besides talking. Luther McCall had the patience of a cougar during the hunt, but he was as edgy as a badger with a sore tooth when it came to just passing time, waiting for something to happen. He glanced over his shoulder. An oversized moon hung bright and full above the horizon. A hunter's moon, he thought. It was going to be a long night.

Luther came awake with a start, senses instantly in tune with his surroundings. It was a trait he'd always had; it took some men an hour and two cups of strong coffee to get their heads out from under their wings, like a goose waking up to a new day. With Luther it was different. One instant he was sound asleep, the next he was wide awake, alert and ready for anything.

He pulled on his shirt and boots, buckled his gun belt around his hips, and reached for his hat. He paused to listen. From the room downstairs, he heard the soft buzz as Amy Caldwell slept. He smiled to himself. One day, maybe, he would mention to Amy that she snored—just to see if she would blush. He doubted it. Amy didn't embarrass all that easily. He picked up his Winchester and let himself out the back way, closing the door silently so as not to awaken her.

The eastern sky held a faint smear of gray as he paused in the alley beside the boardinghouse to watch and listen. He heard nothing out of the ordinary, saw nothing to worry about. His nostrils flared as he tested the breeze; sometimes a man could smell trouble before the other senses picked up any warning signs. Cimarron was as quiet as a church mouse this morning. He thought for a moment about waiting an hour or so before calling on Jimmy and Martha, then dismissed the idea. He had been around Martha Turlock long enough to know she was always up a good two hours before dawn. She was probably reaching for the firewood and the coffeepot by now. A cup of her coffee would be a good start to the day.

Luther smiled as he passed the narrow alley beside the Turlock house. The glow of an oil lamp turned the window of Jimmy's room into a small rectangle of light against the early morning darkness. It was like Martha to check on Jimmy before tending to her own chores and needs, Luther thought. He paused at the front door, wondering if it was still too early to call. He didn't want to catch Martha in her nightdress and possibly embarrass her. Then he decided it wouldn't matter to Martha. He reached out to knock.

The door swung open at the first soft rap of his knuckles. A cold lump formed in Luther's chest. The door should have been bolted at this time of day. He eased the Colt from his holster and thumbed back the hammer, then toed open the door. The front room was empty.

"Martha?"

There was no answer.

Luther slipped into the room, flattened himself against a wall, and listened. A faint sliver of light showed beneath the door to Jimmy's room. He heard a muted sound, like a distant grunt, and the creak of a chair from behind the closed door.

"Martha? Are you all right?"

The sounds stopped.

Luther kept close to the wall as he crept toward Jimmy's door. He nudged the door open with the muzzle of the Winchester—and felt his heart skid in his chest.

"Come in, Travis. Slow and easy."

Otis Holloway stood beside Jimmy's cot, the barrel of the pistol in his hand touching the side of the boy's head. A rag was tied around Jimmy's mouth. Six feet away, Martha Turlock sat bound and gagged, trussed to a straight-backed chair. One of the homesteaders stood behind her. He held a sawed-off double-barreled shotgun to the back of her neck.

Luther took in the scene at a glance and felt the cold lump of anger and helplessness grow. He knew he could put a slug into Holloway's narrow forehead before the storekeeper could pull the trigger. But the shock of the bullet might cause a convulsion of the hand that held the weapon. And that could spatter Jimmy's brains across the room. Even if he managed to take Holloway out, he couldn't nail the nester before the man blew Martha's head off with the smoothbore. Nobody was that fast. Not even Luther McCall. He was trapped.

"Put the pistol down." Holloway's eyes were wide, and his voice trembled. He was nervous and scared, and a frightened man with a gun was twice as dangerous as a man in control of his senses. "Ease the hammer first," Holloway said. "Don't try anything stupid or the kid and the woman die."

Luther did as he was told. He crouched, never taking his gaze from Holloway's close-set eyes, and placed the Colt on the floor.

"Push it over here with your foot."

The pistol skidded across the small room and thumped against a leg of the cot.

"Now the Winchester. Slow and careful."

Luther surrendered the weapon and stood, rage building to a boil in his gut. "What's going on here, Holloway?"

The shopkeeper's thin face cracked in a twisted grin. "Gathering up a little package, friend," he said. The quaver had faded from Holloway's voice. The expression in his eyes was like that of a cat toying with a mouse. "Now, shuck that knife."

Luther eased the blade from its sheath and let it drop. He heard the solid thump as the keen tip buried itself in the worn floorboards. He glanced at the two captives. "Martha, Jimmy—are you all right?"

The two tried to nod. Tears pooled in Martha's green eyes; Jimmy's face was pale, but his chin was held erect and his jaw set. Luther pinned a cold stare through narrowed lids at the shopkeeper. "Holloway, if you've harmed these two, I'll rip your lungs out with my bare hands."

Triumph flickered in Holloway's eyes. "You talk mighty big for a man whose teeth have just been pulled, gun-fighter. I'm going to have myself some fun watching Tyler Scarborough skin you alive."

"So you sold out, you spineless son of a bitch." Luther's voice was heavy and cold. "All right, let's go. Leave Jimmy and Martha alone."

Holloway shook his head. "You're just half the package, Travis. The kid goes with us."

A sharp edge of fear cut through Luther's rage. "You can't take Jimmy along, Holloway. He's not strong enough yet. The ride will kill him."

"Don't matter much whether he lives or dies, as long as Scarborough sees the body. But I'd rather deliver him still breathing. I've got a buckboard out back. We'll put the kid in the back. You'll drive. That way you can't run, and I can keep an eye on you. One wrong move, and you'll be a dead man, Travis—along with the kid." Holloway motioned toward the homesteader. "Lansdale, put the boy in the buckboard."

The homesteader handed his shotgun to Holloway, then lifted Jimmy from the cot. Luther winced as the abrupt motion triggered a whimper of pain from the youth. The man called Lansdale headed for the door. Holloway kept his gun on Jimmy and jerked his head toward the back. "Let's go."

"What about her?" Luther nodded toward Martha Turlock.

"Scarborough's got no need for her. It'll be a while before somebody finds her. By then we'll be miles away." Holloway finally moved the pistol muzzle from Jimmy's head. He gestured toward the back door with the weapon. "Come on. You so much as twitch, I'll blow a hole in the kid."

Luther knew he had no choice at the moment. He glanced at Martha and saw the helplessness and despair reflected in her eyes. "It isn't your fault, Martha," Luther said. He felt the jab of twin shotgun bores in his back and glanced over his shoulder. "You're a dead man, too, Holloway. If I don't kill you, somebody else will. This town won't stand for mistreatment of women and kids, you gutless bastard."

Holloway chuckled. "By the time anybody finds out what's happened around here, Tyler Scarborough and I will own this damned town, friend. Lock, stock, and hitch rail. But you won't be around to see it. Now, *move*."

Luther's mind raced as he walked through the back door, trying to figure a way out. He felt naked and helpless without his weapons. The emptiness in his gut turned colder as he mounted the buckboard and picked up the reins. The mare hitched to the buckboard was old, swaybacked, and rail-thin. She couldn't run a half mile. Even if he tried to whip her into a run, the jostling of the buckboard would most likely kill Jimmy. Two saddled horses waited alongside the buckboard.

Lansdale climbed into the saddle. Holloway handed the shotgun to him. "I'll ride point, Lansdale. You stay in back. If this man so much as hiccups, blow that kid into little pieces." Holloway mounted his own horse, a rangy, big-eared sorrel. "Let's go. Scarborough's waiting to make rich men out of us."

Luther clucked at the old mare and tapped the reins against her rump. She sagged against the traces, and the buckboard creaked into motion. Easy, McCall, Luther silently urged himself. They'll make a mistake somewhere along the way. The trick is to be ready—and to keep Jimmy alive.

CHAPTER
EIGHT

Amy Caldwell stared out the window of the boardinghouse parlor, unable to shake the feeling that something was amiss.

The sun was halfway up the eastern sky, and still there had been no sign of Travis, or of Marshal Josh Turlock. Travis had told her he might be doing a little scouting of the countryside today. Maybe he had already left; he was under no obligation to report his every move to her. His absence at breakfast wasn't that unusual. On several occasions he had been gone from his bed before she arose.

Still, the squirmy sensation in her belly wouldn't go away. She had felt it once before—a full half day before the two cowboys brought Bill's body home, draped across the broad back of one of his draft horses, his blood a dark smear down the sweaty bay's side.

The bandits who attacked the freight wagon and killed her husband and two of his employees had never been found. After four years, Amy still missed Bill Caldwell, his quick smile and gently amorous nature. He lay now in one of the graves in the rocky cemetery outside town. She had sold his half of the grandly named Texas & New Mexico Overland Transport Company. There hadn't been much to sell, just a name and the partly burned hulk of an old Conestoga freighter that had been mostly worn-out when he bought the big wagon.

Bill Caldwell had been a dreamer. The wagon was only the first step, he had told her many times. There would be more wagons, expansion of the lines into Colorado and the Indian Nations. And finally, a share in one of the railroads pushing south from the Union Pacific or feeding the Fort

Worth & Denver line. Then the big house, with servants and half a dozen kids, horses and stables, all the things she had never had and never really hoped to have.

Bill Caldwell's dreams had brought them to this lonely stretch of no-man's-land called the Cimarron Strip. It was, he had said, the last outpost of opportunity for a couple with big plans but only a few dollars in their pockets. They had shared many an evening over wine when they could afford it, simple well water when they didn't have wine, mapping out their future together.

The dreams had died with Bill.

Amy didn't miss the material parts of the dream. She wouldn't have been comfortable around servants anyway, and luxury to her was a decent meal, a hot bath, and a good book. Her needs and wants were simple ones. The income from occasionally rented rooms provided for them. She still idly wondered what it would have been like to have had children. Not a half dozen like Bill wanted, but perhaps a couple. She had often been curious as to what kind of mother she would have been.

Fragments of one dream remained, however. She could still hope that growth and prosperity would eventually come to her town. Amy wasn't exactly sure when Cimarron became *her town*. The lonely community in the middle of nowhere didn't have a lot to offer, but it had grown on her—or she had grown to it, she wasn't sure which. It didn't matter much. It was home.

This morning, it looked more like a ghost town, she thought. The streets were empty except for the occasional tumbleweed that bumped down main street on the freshening west wind. Only the clang of George Winfield's hammer against iron told her there was another soul around Cimarron.

Amy turned away from the window and wandered toward the kitchen. Perhaps, she thought, a cup of tea would chase the queasy sensation from her stomach. Her footsteps seemed to echo in the emptiness of the home she had converted into a boardinghouse. That, in itself, was unusual. Normally she enjoyed the quiet, the solitude, when there were no boarders up and about.

She filled the teakettle from a water pitcher and stirred the coals in the cookstove to life; in a couple of hours it would be too hot in the kitchen to even consider a cup of tea. It had been different when Bill was around. The heat hadn't bothered her then.

Amy fed kindling into the big cast-iron cookstove until she had a small fire going. Maybe, she mused, it had been the simple fact that she had a man about, albeit sometimes underfoot, in the earlier days. She felt no strong urge to repeat the experience. Amy Caldwell had no fear of being alone. She missed Bill, but not men in general. There had been hints at courtship, and more than a few outright lewd suggestions, from boarders over the years. But not since Bill Caldwell had a man appealed to her female instincts.

Until now.

There was something about the man who called himself Travis that seemed to stay at her side even when he was not there. The square shoulders, tousled chestnut hair that seemed always in need of a trim, the almost transparent light blue eyes that brooded most of the time but occasionally flashed with spirit and laughter. He knew the classics of literature, spoke several languages, including Indian tongues—and yet there was a darkness about Travis, a cold violence just below the surface. It was as if he had traveled a lifetime of miles in only a few short years.

The whistle of the kettle broke her reverie. She tried to put thoughts of Travis aside, write them off as feminine curiosity over a man who defied logical analysis. It didn't completely work. She had to admit she was drawn to the man; whether it was long-repressed physical need or a true emotional state, she didn't know. And it didn't matter; he would be moving on soon.

She prepared her tea, sipped it, and winced at the bitter taste it left on her tongue. The knot in her stomach wouldn't even let her enjoy her mid-morning break.

She pushed the teacup aside, banked the fire, and started for the door. There were times for quiet thought and times for action. This morning Amy Caldwell was getting darn tired of thinking.

The wind whipped against her simple, pale blue housedress as she strode down the main street of Cimarron. She
noticed that Otis Holloway hadn't opened the general store
yet, wondered briefly if the man was ill, and decided she
didn't really care. She didn't like Otis Holloway. Never had
and never would.

The door of the Turlock home stood ajar. The knot of
uneasiness tightened in Amy's belly. It wasn't like Martha
to leave the door open on days when the dust blew. Martha
was a meticulous housekeeper.

"Martha?"

There was no answer. Amy stepped inside and closed
the door behind her. "Martha? Jimmy? Is anyone home?"

She heard a muffled sound over the rising moan of the
wind—a human noise, but strange. "Martha? Are you there?"
Amy pushed open the door of Jimmy's room and gasped.
Martha Turlock sat slumped in a chair, bound and gagged,
blood flecked on her upper arms where she had fought the
ropes. Jimmy was nowhere to be seen. The glint of light
on steel caught Amy's eye. A big Damascus knife stood at
the edge of the room, its point buried in the wooden floor.
Travis's knife.

Amy gripped the thick haft of the heavy weapon and
yanked. She had to tug at it twice before it came free. She
darted to Martha's side and sliced the ropes that bound her.
They parted smoothly under the keen blade. She slipped the
blade under the knot of the rag around Martha's face and
sliced through the cloth.

"Martha—are you all right? What happened?"

"They've got Jimmy—and Travis," Martha gasped as the
gag fell away. Tears flooded the lids of her eyes, and her
lower lip trembled.

"Who? Where?"

Martha heaved herself from the chair, stumbled, and
almost fell on legs cramped and weakened from her hours
of bondage. Amy slipped an arm around Martha's waist and
helped her stand erect, then listened in silence as Martha's
story unfolded.

"Where's Josh?"

"Gone out on horseback, scouting. Looking for signs of those outlaws. He said not to expect him back until almost noon." Martha wiped a trembling hand across the tears on her cheeks. "Amy, what are we going to do?" she asked desperately. "Those awful men will kill them both."

Amy released her grip on Martha, satisfied that she could stand without assistance now, and stooped to pick up Travis's revolver and rifle. "I'm going after them, Martha. You stay here until Josh gets back. Tell him what happened."

"Amy, you can't! Even if you catch up, those men will kill you, too!"

"I'll get George to go along." Amy forced a reassuring smile for Martha's benefit. "Don't worry, Martha. We'll get them back."

A half hour later Amy swung into the saddle on a sorrel borrowed from the blacksmith, the heavy Colt pistol tucked into the waistband of hastily donned riding trousers. She led Travis's snorting, nervous brown, saddled and with the Winchester and the big Sharps single-shot thrust into the scabbards. She nodded to the grim-faced blacksmith on the big bay and followed as George Winfield picked up the buckboard tracks at the edge of town. The trail was faint and growing dimmer by the moment as windblown sand whipped around the sparse bunchgrass and sage, covering the tracks of the lightly loaded buckboard. Within a mile the blacksmith had to dismount and study the ground on foot before he picked up the trail again. The tracks led toward the west.

Amy glanced toward a wisp of cloud on the horizon ahead. Please, God, she prayed silently, I've never asked You for much, but now I'm begging. Let Jimmy and Travis live.

Luther McCall winced as the buckboard wheels bounced over a clump of sage, the abrupt jostle bringing a soft moan of pain from the small form in the buckboard bed behind him. The sound fueled the cold, icy rage that swirled in Luther's chest. He knew the boy couldn't take much more abuse. He had to make his move soon.

At least he had a couple of things going for him, despite the obvious odds. The two men who had taken them were rank amateurs when it came to guarding captives; already Luther had noticed a couple of lapses in concentration by the homesteader who rode beside the wagon. The man called Lansdale had made one serious mistake. He had lowered the hammers of the double-barreled shotgun in his hand. It would take him a second to recock the weapon. Luther figured that was all the edge he would need.

Otis Holloway was in the lead, his back to the buckboard. It was now only a matter of time—and timing—Luther knew. And he had a weapon of sorts. With the brightening of the day he had noticed the tip of a buggy whip protruding from beneath the seat. He had quietly and slowly worked it out from under the seat with a toe until it lay beside his right boot. The stiff handle of the whip was broken, but the tough, flexible rawhide thong almost four feet long remained intact. It wasn't much, but it was something.

Luther kept his grinding fury under tight rein as he tried to split his attention between driving the buckboard and watching Holloway and Lansdale. There was no road; they drove over rough terrain, and each jolt of the buckboard brought a soft groan from the boy in back. Luther tried to steer the old mare along the smoothest route possible to lessen Jimmy's pain and the danger of reopening his wound. He hadn't been completely successful.

The buckboard lurched across a shallow, dry creekbed, the old mare straining to heave the rig up the sandy slope on the far side. The mare's nostrils were flared, gasping for air, and lather streaked her bony shoulders and ribs by the time they reached the crest. A few yards beyond, the rocky land abruptly fell into a deeper arroyo.

"Holloway!" Luther called.

The tall man twisted in the saddle to stare at Luther. "What?"

"This mare won't make another mile if you don't call a halt and let her rest for a spell."

The storekeeper shrugged. "I don't give a damn. She can't go, you'll walk and carry the kid. It ain't that far to Horse Springs." The narrow face twisted in a sadistic grin. "After that, it won't matter to you—or the kid." Holloway chuckled and kneed his horse into motion.

The wheezing mare tried to follow, but Luther kept the reins tight. After a moment Holloway disappeared from view beyond the slope of the arroyo, unaware that the others were not close behind. The son of a bitch has just made his last mistake, Luther thought. Time to spring a little trap.

The homesteader with the shotgun reined up alongside the buckboard, almost within arm's reach of Luther. "What the hell's the matter?" Lansdale asked.

"The mare. She's favoring that left hind leg," Luther said. He rose in the seat as if to step from the buckboard. Lansdale waved the shotgun muzzle at Luther. "Stay where you're at, feller," he said. "I'll take a look."

Lansdale lowered the shotgun and reached for the saddle horn, preparing to dismount. It was the instant Luther had been waiting for. He swept the buggy whip from the floor of the buckboard, gripped the handle in one hand and the last foot of the whip end in the other. He crossed his arms to form a loop and dropped the noose over the distracted shotgunner's head in one smooth motion, then he yanked back with all the strength in his two hundred pounds of solid muscle.

The slam of the rawhide garrote against Lansdale's neck sent the shotgun tumbling. Lansdale's horse spooked at the unexpected flash of movement and bolted from beneath the homesteader. A foot hung for an instant in a stirrup; Luther heard the distinct pop as Lansdale's neck broke. He heaved against the rawhide for another few seconds until he was sure Lansdale was dead. The jaded mare danced skittishly in the traces as Luther released the body and leapt from the buckboard. He scooped up the fallen shotgun, cocked back both hammers, and paused for an instant to wrap the mare's off rein securely around his wrist. It wouldn't do to have the mare bolt and bounce Jimmy to death in her last wild run.

Luther stepped in front of the mare and tucked the shotgun stock against his shoulder. An instant later he heard the clatter of hooves. Otis Holloway yanked his horse to a stop at the top of the rise and stared in surprise and shock at the sight that greeted him.

"Good-bye, Otis," Luther said calmly. He pulled both triggers.

The double charge of buckshot caught Holloway full in the chest, lifted him from the saddle, and flung him over his horse's rump into the dust. The shopkeeper's horse bolted. Empty stirrups flapped against the horse's side as it raced back toward Cimarron.

Luther spent a moment calming the buckboard mare, then led the snorting, walleyed animal toward the downed man. He needed only one quick glance to see that Holloway was dead. A double load of buckshot from ten yards did an impressive amount of damage to human flesh.

Luther crouched, retrieved Holloway's Colt, and tucked it into his own gun belt. "Have a nice nap, you sorry son of a bitch," he growled at the broken body in the sand. The killing rage slowly faded. Luther turned to the buckboard.

Jimmy Macko's face was pale and drawn, his eyelids closed, his breathing shallow but regular. The pain of the jostling had finally driven the boy to unconsciousness. It was just as well, Luther knew. At least now the lad wasn't hurting. There was no sign of fresh blood on the bandage over Jimmy's wound. He sighed in relief, then reached out and stroked the harness mare's lathered neck in reassurance. "Sorry, old girl," he said softly, "but it looks like you've got some more work ahead of you. We've got to get Jimmy back home."

He scrounged in the homesteader's pockets and found two more shells for the smoothbore. He broke the action, ejected the spent hulls, and reloaded the weapon. Then he mounted the buckboard and glanced at the sky as he reined the mare about. The position of the sun told Luther it was a few minutes past noon. It would take the rest of the day to get back to Cimarron, he figured. "Hang on, Jimmy," he said. "Fight it. Don't quit on me now."

The mid-afternoon sun sat heavy on Luther McCall's back, its heat compounded by the blast furnace wind. Dust devils danced in the scrub brush and parched prairie grass. The blazing sun played tricks on the eyes and mind, painting cool lake waters on the distant horizon and then yanking them away as the buckboard neared, a cruel trick dealt to tongues parched with thirst.

The only canteens had been on the horses ridden by Holloway and Lansdale, and the two animals were long gone. Once, Luther thought he had found water—a slow seep in the bank of a dry creek. But the water was useless, too heavily laden with gypsum for human consumption. It had slaked the harness mare's thirst, but Luther knew that a single cupful of the stuff would tie a man's guts in knots for days. The Cimarron had drinkable water, but it lay three miles to the south through rugged, broken country all but impassable by buckboard.

Luther could bear the growing thirst himself. He was accustomed to long, dry trails. Normally he could focus his mind on some real but distant, or even imagined, object and suppress the body's constant cry for water. But Jimmy was suffering the agonies of the damned. The young body needed water to repair itself, and none was to be had. The boy had awakened two hours ago and asked weakly for water. When Luther told him there was none to be had, Jimmy didn't whine or beg. He accepted the discomfort and the pain of his wound in stoic silence. The boy is twelve going on thirty, Luther mused. Not many grown men could go through this without whimpering.

Luther's hand slapped against the receiver of the shotgun as he spotted movement beyond the heat waves that danced along the trail. The metal of the smoothbore was almost hot enough to burn. Luther eased the mare over to the cover of a stand of twisted and stunted mesquites. The thin cover wasn't much, but it was all they had, and at least the wind-whipped branches of thorns and dried beans would break up the outline of the buckboard.

"What . . . is it, Travis?" Jimmy's words were hard to make out. The voice was weak and the words slurred from lips thickened with thirst.

"Two riders coming, Jimmy," Luther said softly. He cocked the right barrel of the shotgun. "Looks like three horses. Stay quiet. We're too close to home to take any chances now."

Luther squinted through the whorls of dust for several minutes, then sighed in relief as the lead rider drew close enough to recognize. "It's George Winfield, Jimmy. Looks like he's following the tracks we made going out." Luther stared hard at the second rider before recognition hit him like an almost physical blow. "Amy Caldwell's with him. Let's go, son." He lowered the hammer of the shotgun and tapped the reins against the rump of the jaded mare.

The riders kicked their mounts into a lope as the buckboard came into view. Moments later Winfield and Amy pulled up alongside. Luther noted with satisfaction that they had brought Chili along, saddled and ready to go, with both his rifles in their scabbards and his saddlebags in place.

"Thank God," Amy said. "Are you all right, Travis? Jimmy?"

"A touch on the thirsty side," Luther answered, "but otherwise we're in pretty good shape, considering what might have been."

Amy all but leapt from the saddle, a canteen in hand, and clambered onto the buckboard. She cradled the boy's head in her lap and held the canteen to his lips. "Not too much all at once, Jimmy," she said. "Just a few sips now. Later you can drink your fill."

"What happened, Travis? You managed to get away from those two?" Winfield asked.

Luther smiled. "You might say that."

Winfield glanced around, his ancient .44 rimfire Henry rifle at the ready. "Where'd they go?"

"To hell, I expect. They won't be any more trouble." Luther's tone was calm and flat. "Their bodies are back there a few miles."

Amy handed the canteen over her shoulder. Luther took a swig. The water was tepid but sweet to the tongue. He sloshed it around his mouth before swallowing. He waited for the initial sip to ease the most painful ache of thirst, then took two swallows before handing the canteen back.

"We were afraid we'd find you both dead, Travis," Amy said. "It's such a relief to find you alive."

"How's Jimmy?" There was genuine concern in Winfield's voice.

"I think he'll be all right," Amy said. "There's no fresh bleeding. The wound didn't break open." Luther glanced around. Amy was stroking the boy's tousled, sandy hair. The back of her hand was beginning to turn red from the sun. "Did you kill them both, Travis?"

Luther nodded. "I didn't have any other choice." He didn't elaborate.

Amy didn't shudder or wince. She surprised Luther. "Serves the bastards right," she said. "Picking on a sick boy like this . . ." Her voice trailed away.

Luther climbed from the buckboard seat and handed the reins to the blacksmith. "I'd appreciate it if you'd see Amy and Jimmy back to Cimarron, George," he said.

Winfield raised an eyebrow. "What about you?"

Luther reached for Chili's reins. "I found out where Tyler Scarborough's bunch is—or will be. Place called Horse Springs. You know it?"

The blacksmith nodded, then raised a thick finger. "See that peak yonder? The one that looks a little like a saddle? Horse Springs is in a canyon two miles south of that, halfway between the peak and the river."

"I'll find it." Luther tugged the cinch tight on Chili and toed the stirrup.

"Travis, what are you going to do?" Luther heard the note of alarm in Amy's question.

"I'm going to Horse Springs." His tone was cold, the words tight.

"Travis," Winfield said solemnly, "you can't take on that whole gang by yourself." He gripped the receiver of the Henry hard enough to whiten his knuckles. "I'm going with you."

"No. Thanks for the offer, George, but I work best alone. I'm going to cut the odds down some. Delay them at Horse Springs a while, with luck. That will give Marshal Turlock time to gather his forces. He'll need your help."

Amy climbed from the buckboard as Luther swung into the saddle. She put a hand on his leg. "Travis, do you have to do this? You should come back with us, maybe get some help."

Luther's face twisted in a scowl. "I won't need help just yet, Amy," he said. "Those men have tried to kill Jimmy twice. They almost killed you when that one tried to bushwhack me. It's personal now. And the more snakes I can stomp now, the less of a chance other people will get bitten later."

Amy's hand fell away. Her shoulders seemed to slump. Luther noticed that her slight sunburn emphasized the row of freckles across her nose and cheekbones. She looked, he thought, like a sixteen-year-old girl instead of a woman grown. He forced a smile. "Don't worry about me, Amy. I know what I'm doing. You just make sure Jimmy gets home all right."

She nodded and wiped a windblown strand of hair from her mouth. "Your knife is in the saddlebag. I thought you might need it. I checked. There's extra ammunition, too."

Luther touched fingers to his hat brim in thanks and started to rein Chili away. "Wait a minute," Amy said. She picked up the canteen and gave it a shake. "Take this. It's about half full. George has another one. We won't need more than that before we get back home."

Luther lashed the canteen to his saddle and touched heels to Chili's ribs. The horse pranced and snorted, then apparently decided it was too hot to pitch. The hump in the brown's back flattened out, and he moved out at a brisk trot. Luther didn't look back. He squinted against the wind toward the saddle-shaped peak, mentally calculating the distance. He could reach the peak an hour before sunset without pushing Chili too hard and be close to the place called Horse Springs by dark.

"All right, Scarborough, you son of a bitch," he muttered to himself, "you just bought yourself into a war."

CHAPTER
NINE

Tyler Scarborough squatted on his heels beside the small camp fire near the edge of the wide, shallow pool known as Horse Springs.

Something about the place made Tyler nervous, but he couldn't pin down exactly what.

Even in full daylight, the canyon campsite didn't feel right. Now, with faint wisps of clouds drifting across the face of a moon just past full, it felt worse. The canyon was deep and narrow, barely two hundred yards across at its widest point. Sheer walls flanked two sides of the twisting canyon, almost vertical in most places and studded with heavy clumps of juniper and dense cedar trees amid massive knots of sandstone boulders that appeared tossed about like huge dice thrown by a drunken gambler.

The floor of the canyon was as smooth and even as the sides were rough and steep, and almost without cover. Over the years campers at the site from Indians to buffalo hunters to sheepherders and cowboys had stripped all but a few cottonwood trees from the stand of timber that had lined the spring and its narrow, whispering creek that twisted south toward the Cimarron. A few large sandstone boulders had tumbled from the sheer walls above onto the canyon floor. The smattering of big rocks and trees was the only solid cover for those camped in the canyon.

Scarborough fished a thin Mexican cigarillo from his pocket and fired the smoke with a twig from the camp fire. He drew in a deep breath of the heavy tobacco and listened intently to the night sounds along the canyon.

In the near distance a coyote's staccato yelps faded into a long, mournful wail. The silhouette of a hunting owl flashed on silent wings past the high round moon. The rip of horses grazing the strip of rich green grass along the spring-fed creek and the snores of men in their bedrolls seemed loud in the night air. The wind had stopped at sundown, and an eerie stillness had settled over Horse Springs. The whole layout was, to Scarborough's thinking, one spooky place. He could almost feel the ghosts of travelers past staring at him from perches high on the rugged bluffs overlooking the camp. Tyler had his lookouts posted, one man on the east canyon wall and another on the west. They would stand four-hour watches before being relieved, and so far there had been no alarm sounded by the pickets. That didn't reassure Scarborough much. This place just felt like trouble.

Scarborough tried to tell himself his uneasiness was because there had been no sign of Otis Holloway and his partner, the homesteader. They were a good twelve hours overdue, and Scarborough couldn't shake the feeling they weren't coming. He grunted in disgust and dragged on the cigarillo. If something had happened to the Cimarron storekeeper and his down-at-heel buddy, it was no skin off Tyler's nose. He was going to kill the two anyway, as soon as they delivered that Travis fellow and the kid. But their not showing up meant one of two things, neither of them good. Either the two had turned chicken and not tried to take the man who had gunned down Dolph—or they had grabbed him and found out they couldn't turn loose. Either way, the big man was still in Cimarron. They would have to dig him out the hard way.

Tyler wasn't all that worried about the man called Travis. He had picked up three more seasoned gun hands from the Raton saloons, and he now had sixteen men under his command. They would go through Cimarron like crap through a goose. Two days after taking over the town, Tyler and a half dozen handpicked men would be on their way to make a withdrawal from the Trail City bank. The Southwest was about to see the founding of a Robber's Roost that would make the Hole in the Wall country seem like a Sunday school picnic spot. He told himself he didn't have a thing to worry about. Not a thing—

Tyler started—his hand grabbing for the butt of the .41 Lightning—at the soft crunch of sand beneath foot at his back. He drew and turned in one quick motion, then grumbled a curse at the figure behind him.

"Dammit, Moondog," Scarborough snapped, "don't ever sneak up on me like that. I came damn close to poking a hole in your Apache gut." He holstered the Lightning.

The Indian ignored the scolding. He squatted by the fire and stared toward the distant disk that played tag with the clouds. After several moments, Moondog glanced up at Scarborough. "You feel it, too?"

Scarborough snorted in disdain. He would never admit to being spooked—not to this superstitious Apache. "Feel what?"

"Bad spirit. Out there. Close." Moondog lifted his gaze again to the eastern canyon bluff.

"Bad spirit, my butt," Scarborough groused. "You been chewing that damn peyote again, Moondog?"

The Apache shook his head. "No medicine buttons. Don't need peyote to feel bad spirits. The Moon Wolf hunts tonight. I feel him."

Scarborough muttered an oath of disgust. "You and that damn wolf of yours are going to drive me loco. There's no such thing as bad spirits and moon wolves."

"Maybe." Moondog rose to his feet, sniffing the wind. "Maybe not. We see."

"Since you're still up, Moondog," Scarborough said, "you might as well go relieve Carlos. His watch is about over." Scarborough waggled a finger at the Apache. "Don't you go seein' any ghosts out there, either. If you start yellin' at shadows, I'll feed you to that Moon Wolf of yours myself."

The Apache nodded silently and strode toward the rocky crags of the eastern bluff. The Indian's body seemed to merge with the shadows before he had taken a dozen strides; one moment he was there, in plain view, and the next moment he was gone. Scarborough sighed and squatted back beside the coals of the dying fire. The Apache's words had shaken him more than Tyler Scarborough wanted to admit. The damn peyote eater feels it, too, Tyler thought; I'm not the only one jumpy tonight. I'll be damn glad to leave this place tomorrow.

On the east side of the canyon, Luther McCall crouched beneath the low limbs of an aged, wind-twisted juniper and stared toward the distant glow of camp fire coals. His muscles were relaxed, his senses tuned to the night. Every sound, every smell, every movement in the camp below seemed magnified in the still night air.

He had crouched motionless beneath the juniper, moving nothing but his eyes, for more than five hours. He wondered if this was how the cougar felt in the closing stalk of the hunt.

It hadn't taken long to determine the routine of the outlaw band. Two pickets, one on each canyon wall, their locations marked by the flare of a match, a soft cough, or the stream of liquid as a sentry relieved himself. A fresh set of eyes came on duty every four hours.

Luther heard the rustle of juniper leaves against cloth, the soft, muted voices less than twenty feet away, as the watch changed. The new man on sentry duty was the Indian. Luther had watched the man with interest from the time Scarborough's bunch had first ridden into the Horse Springs canyon two hours before sunset. The man's clothing and bearing marked him as Apache; he had the mannerisms of a warrior, an unspoken tension about him, the look of a snake already coiled and ready to strike without sounding a warning rattle. One of the dangerous ones.

Luther would let the Apache live through the night. He didn't plan to make his move until the last sentry change before dawn. At that time of day the camp would be deep in sleep; before the outlaws discovered what the night had brought, the rising sun would be lightening the eastern sky.

It would be good shooting light, soft but bright enough to pick targets, and the rising sun would be in the eyes of the men in the camp.

Luther waited another hour, then silently slid from beneath the juniper and started the mile-long stalk around the north end of the canyon. The sentry on the west side would have to be the first to fall.

Amy Caldwell came awake with a start, unsure for a moment what had jarred her from an unplanned doze in the straight-backed chair beside Jimmy's cot. The quick surge of anxiety faded as Josh Turlock poked his leathery face through the doorway.

"Everything all right in here, Amy?" the marshal asked, his voice little more than a whisper.

Amy glanced at the boy. He seemed to be sleeping peacefully, the smooth face free of any pain lines. "I think so," she said softly. "There hasn't been any bleeding. He's been asleep for quite a while now."

The marshal limped into the room, leaning on his cane. Amy saw that he had the old Remington .44 holstered at his hip. It was unlike Josh Turlock to carry a firearm in his own house. But then, she reminded herself, these were not normal times.

"I'll take over here, Amy," Turlock said. "I can't sleep anyway, and you need some rest." The marshal glanced toward the window above Jimmy's cot. "It'll be daylight in a couple of hours. If you like, you can nudge Martha over and catch some sleep in our bed."

Amy flexed her shoulders to banish the fatigue from her muscles. Sitting in a hard chair most of the night was not the most comfortable way to spend an evening. "How's Martha?" she asked.

Josh Turlock's smile lifted the ends of the thick, bushy handlebar mustache. "Sleeping like a tired hound," he said. "She was worn down. More tired in the head from worry than anything else, I think. She'll be fine when the rooster crows."

Amy nodded and reached for her light shawl. "I'll go back to my own bed, Marshal," she said. "No need to risk disturbing Martha."

The grandfatherly smile faded from the old man's face. "I'd rather you stayed here, Amy," he said. "We don't know what's going to happen today. I'd sort of like to keep you where I can watch over you for a spell."

Amy reached out and placed a hand on the marshal's forearm. "Don't concern yourself with me, Josh," she said. "You've a wife and a wounded boy to watch over—and a town to protect. I'll be fine. I'll have a loaded shotgun by the bed." She tossed the shawl over her shoulder and turned toward the door, then hesitated. "Josh, Travis said he was going to carry the fight to those outlaws, slow them down some. I'm worried about him. One man, against all those guns. . . ." Her voice trailed away.

The expression in Josh Turlock's eyes turned cold. "I don't think you need to worry about Travis," he said. "He knows what he's doing. I don't think I'd want to be in Tyler Scarborough's camp right now."

"Josh, what will we do if Travis doesn't come back?"

The marshal sighed. "I don't know about you, Amy, but I know what I'll do. Go ahead with setting up our defenses. George Winfield's out on top of the river breaks now, watching the trails into town. They won't catch us by surprise."

Amy's brow wrinkled in a frown. "Can we stop them, Josh? Realistically, do we have a chance?"

Josh Turlock's mustache twitched in a frown. "I can't say. The odds don't look good right now. If anybody wants to make a bet with you, put your money on the Scarborough gang. But we'll give them a fight, at least."

Amy's eyes narrowed and a muscle twitched along her jawline. "Count me in on the defensive force, Josh. I can handle a shotgun."

Turlock shook his head. "I can't have a woman risk her life doing a man's job. If they get past me and the others, God knows what they'd do to you."

"They'd do it anyway." Amy's tone was calm but determined. "And if they're going to do it, they'll have to be content with doing it to a dead woman. I'm going to fight them, Josh. Tell me what to do as long as you let me help, but don't ask me to stay out of it."

The marshal stared at Amy for a moment. "If I order you to stay away from the fighting?"

"I'll ignore your order. I've heard you say this is your town. It's mine, too. I'm not going to stand by and wring my hands like some helpless female when my town is under siege."

Josh Turlock smiled. "I believe you. I don't think I could stop you short of putting you in irons." His voice was tinged with admiration. "You're quite a woman, Amy Caldwell."

Amy inclined her blond head. "I will take that as a compliment, Marshal." She glanced out the window. The sky was showing the first gray light of false dawn. "I must say I hope Travis gets back here safely, and for more than just"—she flushed slightly—"personal reasons. I know you don't care much for him. There's an obvious tension between the two of you. You're suspicious of him. But, Marshal, we need Travis when those men come."

Josh Turlock's eyes narrowed. "I am, and we do. He's a gunman. We aren't. I have to tell you this: If we survive this fight that's coming, Travis won't be needed in my town any longer. I'm going to ask him to move on."

Amy ran a hand through her hair. "I don't think you should," she said calmly. "I suspect he'll move on of his own accord—and I'm afraid that if you try to push him, he'll push back. I don't want to lose either of you." She turned away and strode through the door into the lingering darkness.

Josh Turlock listened as Amy's footsteps faded and closed the door softly behind her. Then he limped to the east window and stared into the darkness. Girl, he told her in his mind, for your sake, don't get involved with that man. I know who he is, and he's not for you.

The thought brought a knowing smile to the marshal's lips. "And I've got a feeling," he muttered softly, "that Tyler Scarborough and his bunch are about to find out something about this man who calls himself Travis. I don't think they're going to like it all that much."

Luther McCall stood behind the aged juniper on the west side of Horse Springs Canyon and listened to the rustle of clothing as the sentry shifted his weight.

For the last five minutes, Luther had stood close enough to the sentry to smell the man. It was obvious that the stocky, thick-chested outlaw was a few miles south of his last bath. Luther crept a step closer, his movements silent in the pre-dawn air. The sentinel carried a holstered pistol on his hip and a thin skinning knife in a sheath on his belt. And he was bored. His rifle rested against a fork in the juniper, all but lost in the black shadows cast by the dim light of the lowering moon.

Luther had never seen the man before, but he had no qualms about killing a total stranger. Especially when the man was one of those trying to kill him. The key to survival in a war was to kill the enemy first. And this was a war, one man against many. The outlaw had picked his own trail to ride. He probably deserved killing on general principles.

Luther waited patiently, feeling the steady, controlled pulse of his heart against his ribs. Time wasn't a matter of concern yet; the outlaw still had almost three hours left on his watch before the camp in the canyon stirred to life.

The sentinel stepped away from the trunk of the tree, fiddled with his trouser buttons, and began to relieve himself against a nearby boulder. Luther waited until he heard the man's sigh of relief and the steady splash of urine against the boulder. He knew he would never get a better chance. A man taking a leak had only one thing on his mind at the time.

Luther took one more silent step as he eased the heavy Damascus knife from its sheath. He was less than two feet behind the sentry now. The steady stream of urine faded to short pulses as the broad-shouldered outlaw forced the last of the fluid from his bladder. Luther reached out with his left hand, clamped a big palm across the sentry's mouth, yanked his head back, and ripped the Damascus knife upward. The blade snagged for an instant as the keen tip dug into a rib. The outlaw cried out in pain and shock, the sound a strangled grunt against Luther's hand. Luther twisted his shoulders and heaved against the haft of the Damascus. The blade ripped free of the rib and sank to the hilt, the tip driving up between the ribs toward the soft organs above. The panicked outlaw grabbed at the hand over his mouth and tried to twist away, then bucked his body back against Luther's chest. Luther twisted the knife blade. The man's struggles weakened rapidly until his body went limp. Luther held him erect for a moment, then yanked the knife free. The outlaw died with a soft gurgle, drowned in his own blood from the lung ravaged by the big knife blade. Luther let the body slump toward the ground as he wiped the Damascus blade on the dead man's shoulder.

He sheathed the knife, dragged the man to the trunk of the tree where he had been standing watch, and propped the body in a sitting position against the big juniper. He leaned the dead man's rifle against the body and stepped back, satisfied. If anyone should happen to walk up on the sentry post, it would appear at first glance that the outlaw had merely fallen asleep. It was not likely anyone would come until the man's watch ended, but Luther took nothing for granted. Sometimes a few seconds meant the difference between life and death in this game.

Luther turned and slipped back into the boulders and brush of the canyon wall. So far, so good, he thought. One down, one more to go before sunrise.

Twenty yards from the dead sentry's post, Luther quickened his pace.

An hour later he was back on the east side of the canyon, the big Sharps and the smaller Winchester cradled in an arm as he neared the second sentinel's post. Fifty feet from the lookout point he knelt and placed the two rifles carefully on the ground, positioned so that he could scoop them up on the run if necessary. Satisfied with his preparations, he began his second stalk of the morning.

Luther eased his way belly-down through a clump of Spanish dagger and silently breathed a curse as he started toward the sentry. This man knew what he was doing. He stood with his back against a big sandstone boulder, alert and watchful, the shaggy, bearded head moving slowly from side to side as his gaze swept the countryside. Luther held his breath as the sentry seemed to stare straight at him, then breathed in relief. The man hadn't noticed him in the deep shadows of the Spanish dagger patch.

Luther studied the swath of sandy, rocky terrain between himself and the sentinel. There seemed to be no way to cover the last ten feet without crossing open ground, and it would be all but impossible to flank the man; his position against the boulder left him protected from attack from behind. Luther cast a quick glance at the sky. The moon rode low against the horizon on the west, and a pale predawn light washed the eastern skyline. He knew he had to do something, and soon. Time was working against him now. In little more than a quarter hour the outlaw camp would begin to stir. He had to be in position by then, and that meant taking this man down quickly.

Luther mentally checked off his options. It didn't take long. He wasn't prepared to risk a gunshot and awaken the outlaw camp—not yet. He couldn't get behind the man for a silent ambush. That left only one approach, and it was a chancy one. But it was the only one he had.

Luther squirmed from beneath the Spanish dagger, waited until the sentry's gaze had swept past again, then wriggled into a shallow wash on his right. He crouched, waiting and listening, for a few heartbeats, then made his way down the steep slope of the canyon wall. He winced as his foot dislodged a bit of shale and sent it whispering down the canyon wall. But the sound went unchallenged.

A few minutes later, Luther stood upright in the narrow trail leading from the outlaw camp below to the lookout point. It was the one direction the sentry wouldn't be concerned about. Luther took a deep breath, loosened the Colt in its holster, and strode toward the outpost. He made no attempt to keep his approach silent.

Luther stepped around the boulder. The sentry turned, his thumb on the uncocked hammer of the rifle in his hands.

"Mornin'," Luther said casually. "Tyler wants you. Sent me to take over. Everything quiet?"

Up close, Luther could make out the features behind the beard and untrimmed hair that tumbled from beneath a battered felt hat. The lookout had a broad chest, thick arms, and a weathered face. He had the look of a man who knew how to use that rifle in his hands.

"What's he want?"

"Beats me. Didn't say."

The sentry stared for a few heartbeats at Luther. "I don't know you, mister," he said, his tone wary and suspicious. His thumb tightened on the hammer of the rifle.

Luther knew it was now or never. He slammed his left fist into the leathery face and felt the cartilage crumple under the blow. The sentry staggered back, stunned, the rifle almost falling from his grasp. Luther whipped the Colt Peacemaker from his holster and slammed the heavy pistol against the side of the man's head. The sentry went down hard. Luther cracked the Colt against his head again. The bearded man's body went limp under the second blow.

Luther stood for a moment over the unconscious outlaw, breathing harder than he expected. It had been close. Then he holstered the Colt, knelt behind the man's head, slipped a hand underneath his shoulders, and pulled his slack form partly upright. "Sorry, old-timer," Luther said softly, "but I can't risk you waking up. McCall's Second Law of Survival: no second chances." He tucked the thumb side of his left forearm against the sentry's neck, placed his right palm against the man's head, and shoved.

The sentry's neck snapped with an audible crack.

Luther quickly rose and hurried back to where he had left his two rifles. The sky was brightening fast now. Cradling the weapons in his arms, he strode rapidly to the point he had chosen as his ambush site—a flat open space at the lip of the canyon wall which provided a clear view of the camp below.

Luther settled in behind the opening, checked his weapons a final time, and again calculated the distance from his post to the outlaw camp fire. He made it a few steps over four hundred yards. An easy shot with the big Sharps Fifty, but out of efficient range of the .44-40 Winchester. Too bad the Sharps folks don't make a repeater, he mused; I could take out half that camp with a big-bore lever action.

Luther cocked the Winchester and placed it beside him within easy reach, then hefted the Sharps. He flipped up the bar sight on the tang of the weapon and clicked the bar into its third notch. He knew from long experience with the Fifty that the third notch was four hundred yards—and that the big-bore rifle put its heavy slug dead on target if the shooter did his job. He didn't have to worry about wind drift. The morning air was still.

He aligned the blade of the front sight in the shallow

"V" of the rear target sight and peered down the barrel of the Sharps toward the outlaw camp below.

Most of the men still slept. A few were beginning to stir in the soft gray light. A small, wiry man crouched beside the fire, feeding wood into a trickle of smoke. Luther swung the muzzle about the camp. He didn't see the Apache who had come on watch earlier and felt a twinge of disappointment. Luther had hoped to take the Indian down from ambush. When hunting wild hogs, a man put the most dangerous boar down first. It saved a lot of worry later on.

Luther held his fire as the camp sluggishly woke to the new day. The light was growing better by the moment; in another ten minutes it would be perfect for long-range rifle work. A few men picked up saddles and headed for the horses picketed at the north edge of the camp. Luther smiled grimly to himself. He had a little trap planned for anybody who chased him. It looked like he might hook himself a few fish in that rockfall up the canyon. He ignored the men headed for the horses. He would worry about them later.

A sudden yelp from the far side of the canyon brought a silent curse to Luther's lips. The body of the first sentry had been found. He couldn't wait that ten minutes now. He snugged the Sharps against his shoulder and lined the sights on the man who had been tending the fire and now stood, staring toward the canyon wall. Luther started to squeeze the trigger, sensing the delicate balance of sear and hammer spring—then stopped before the hammer tripped.

A man who had scrambled from his blankets stepped between Luther and his chosen target, the short man at the fire. Luther hesitated only a split second. He knew he had to open this dance now, before Scarborough's band got organized or scattered. He tugged the final quarter ounce of tension from the trigger.

The big rifle slammed against Luther's shoulder, spouting a dense ball of powder smoke and a bright muzzle flash. For a half second that seemed an eternity, Luther saw and heard nothing but the muzzle blast of the big Fifty. Then the smoke thinned; the man Luther had in his sights seemed to jump into the air, arms flailing. He fell into the small man and both went down. Luther had no way of knowing whether the Sharps slug had passed through the man it had hit and struck the second. He didn't have time to wait and find out. Startled cries sounded from the camp.

Luther lowered the Sharps and swept the Winchester to his shoulder. He slapped off three quick shots, not aiming, not really hoping to hit anything but giving the men in camp something to fret over. Then he scooped up the Sharps and sprinted thirty feet to his left. He dropped onto his belly and reloaded the Sharps.

He heard the spat and whine as slugs fired from the camp hammered into the hillside before the sound of the rifle reports reached his ears. The slugs fell well short of where Luther had been, his former location still marked by the smear of powder smoke from his two weapons. The repeating rifles carried by the men in camp could not accurately reach the lip of the canyon. Luther calmly drew in a breath, let it out slowly as he lined the Sharps sights on a man near the edge of the camp, and squeezed the trigger. The big Fifty thundered again; a second later the heavy slug slammed the man onto his back. Luther whipped the Winchester to his shoulder and sent three slugs arcing toward a man running toward the horses tethered at a picket line. The man stumbled, but quickly regained his footing.

Luther levered two more .44-40 rounds into the camp. The men had already scattered, crouching behind whatever cover they could find—saddles, wood gathered to feed the fire, even the bodies of their downed comrades. Luther reloaded the Sharps. He drew a bead as a rifle barrel poked from behind a saddle. He saw the puff of smoke from the outlaw's rifle as he squeezed the Sharps trigger. The saddle bounced as the big slug slammed through the wood and leather. Luther heard the cry of pain from behind the saddle. The rifle fell.

"Can't hide from a Sharps Fifty behind a saddle, friend," Luther muttered as he reloaded. Puffs of dust kicked up from the canyon wall beneath him as more of the outlaws pointed rifles toward their unseen attacker. The slugs were walking up the hill as the gunmen began to find the range. Luther scooped up his Winchester and slithered away from the lip of the canyon, then came to his feet and sprinted toward the brush-choked gully two hundred yards away where Chili was tied.

Minutes later he stood beside the snorting brown, thumbed fresh cartridges into the Winchester's loading port, reloaded the Sharps, stowed both rifles in their scabbards, and toed the stirrup. As he swung into the saddle, he heard the distant yells from the outlaw camp, then the rumble of hooves. He reined the brown toward the saddle-backed peak to the north. "Time to get out of here, Chili," he said as the brown broke into a run. "One of those jaspers might get a lucky slug in one of us."

Luther gave Chili his head for the run up-canyon toward the peak. The brown was strong, fast and surefooted, and had more endurance than any horse Luther had ever owned. Luther wasn't concerned about being run down. The speedy gelding gained ground on the pursuing horses with almost every stride.

After a mile, Chili thundered through the narrow pass in a jumble of boulders that almost closed off the canyon trail. Luther had noted the spot on the ride to Horse Springs. He pulled Chili to a sliding stop fifty yards beyond the boulder fall, slid the Winchester from its scabbard, and dismounted. He cracked the action to make sure a cartridge was chambered and led Chili into the willow thicket beside the canyon wall. The brown was breathing hard, but far from winded. Luther cocked an ear toward the sounds of pursuit. He made it four riders. The others would be quite a ways behind. It took a surprised and spooked man a spell to get his wits about him enough to figure out what was going on and start to fight back.

Luther looped Chili's reins around his right arm, knelt, and cocked the Winchester.

The first two riders pounded around the rockfall, almost stirrup to stirrup. Luther drew a quick bead and squeezed the trigger. The rider on the left snapped erect in the stirrups, then tumbled from the saddle. The second rider tried to bring his rifle into line and managed a wild shot before Luther's second round hammered into his chest. Two horses, saddles now empty, sped past Luther and raced off.

The third pursuer charged into the open, handgun at the ready. Luther snapped a quick shot and grunted in disgust as the slug missed its mark. He worked the action of the Winchester. The fourth man didn't show; apparently he had pulled up when the firing started in front of him. Luther remounted and touched heels to Chili's ribs.

A rifle slug buzzed past Luther's ear as Chili lowered his head in a flat-out run. Luther glanced over his shoulder. The fourth man stood atop a boulder, rifle at his shoulder. Luther kneed Chili abruptly to the left and heard the whack of the rifleman's slug into the ground. Then Chili slid down the bank of a shallow, dry creek, and a few strides later rounded a sharp bend in the creekbed.

Luther checked the brown, pulling him back to an easy lope as the danger from behind faded. Anyone coming up that canyon now would do so with care, Luther knew. Any thinking man got a mite cautious when he knew he could ride into an ambush at any step. And after losing that many men in such a short time Scarborough's bunch would be more than a little cautious.

Luther reined Chili along the path taken by the fleeing horses of the two men he'd shot at the boulders. The flight of the horses was an unexpected but welcome bonus. Chili's hoofprints would mix with those of the outlaw horses until it would take an expert tracker to untangle the trail.

Luther squinted toward the saddle-shaped peak in the near distance, its upper half bathed now in bright sunlight. He would leave enough of a trail to lure the outlaws into thinking he'd make a stand at the peak, then double back and head for Cimarron. Covering a trail was second nature to him by now. When the outlaws finally figured out he wasn't on the peak, he'd be back in Cimarron— and today he had cost Scarborough time and men.

Luther pulled Chili back to a trot. There was no need to run the tough brown into the ground. He wanted to keep a bit of reserve strength and speed in Chili, just in case something went wrong.

Three hours later Luther was back on the trail to Cimarron. Any pursuit was far behind now. Luther found himself whistling silently.

It had been a good day.

CHAPTER
TEN

Josh Turlock leaned against the corner of the blacksmith shop and stared along the valley that carried the rutted road west from Cimarron.

There was no sign of movement along the road except for an occasional tumbleweed struggling to pull strength from the light west wind and the gentle quaver of cottonwood leaves along the riverbed.

Josh blinked against the sandy feeling in his eyelids. He had managed but two hours of sleep in the past day and a half. His leg still hurt from the unaccustomed long hours in the saddle on a scout that yielded nothing. But except for the occasional blurring of vision that was beginning to fade with the passing years, he felt little need for rest. Only good thing about getting long in the tooth, he thought, is that a man doesn't need near as much sleep as a young flat-bellied buck.

"See anything yet, Josh?"

The marshal cast a quick glance at George Winfield. The blacksmith stood in the doorway of his shop, sweat streaming down his broad face as he wiped callused hands on a bit of soiled cloth. Winfield's .44 Henry leaned against the door. He had the Colt Dragoon strapped around his hips in a worn military holster and cartridge belt.

Josh shook his head. "Nothing yet." He glanced at the sun. It was more than halfway across the western sky.

"You reckon Travis got himself shot or caught?"

"Maybe. I wouldn't bet on it either way." The marshal turned his head and spat, then reached for the battered pipe in his vest pocket. "Even if Scarborough's bunch did put him down, he bought us some time, or they would have

been here by now. It's not that long a ride to Horse Springs.
With luck, maybe Travis cut the odds down some."

Winfield grunted. "Not that it's going to do us all that
much good, Josh. I'm not sure this town can stand up to
a bunch of gunfighters."

Josh tamped tobacco into the pipe bowl and reached for
a match. He cocked an eyebrow at Winfield. "You getting
cold feet on me, George?"

Winfield winced. "You know better than that, Josh. I'll
be here when the shooting starts. A couple others have got
a little limp in the backbone department, though."

"Braden one of 'em?"

"Yeah. Heard Braden tell Denver Smith he wasn't sure
a cook was supposed to sling lead instead of spuds."

Josh fired the pipe and grimaced at the bitter taste of
raw burley on his tongue. "What did Smith say to that?"

The blacksmith chuckled. "Thought that old cowboy
turned beer pusher was going to crawl Braden's frame
right there. Wasn't exactly complimentary, what he had
to say." Winfield's smile faded. "Clem Barnes quit us, too.
Just saddled up and rode out."

The marshal squinted through the pipe smoke at Winfield.
"No surprise there. Lots of folks talk big until time to get
shot at comes close. Back in the war we had a lot of fellows
desert the day before a battle. It's the waiting that grinds
down their nerves."

Winfield sighed. "Mine, too," he said. "I don't know how
good a fight we can put up. I wish we had Travis here. We
could sure use his guns."

"You've got them."

The voice from behind caused both men to start. Winfield
whirled, his hand on the butt of the old Dragoon. Luther
McCall stood at the far corner of the blacksmith shop, two
rifles casually resting across a shoulder.

"Damn, Travis," Winfield grumbled as his hand fell away
from the Dragoon, "you shouldn't sneak up on a man like
that. Near caused me to wet my britches."

Luther smiled. "Guess I'm in the habit of traveling
quiet."

"Where the hell did you come from? Josh has been watching the west road since way before noon."

Luther shrugged. "Found a deer trail down the north river bluff wall." He jabbed a thumb over his shoulder. "Take care of Chili for me, George? I'd do it myself, but I need a little war parley with the marshal."

Turlock waited until George Winfield disappeared around the corner, then leveled a steady stare at Luther. "What happened out there, Travis?"

"Tyler Scarborough's boys got a little touch of snakebite. They'll be mad as hell now. How's Jimmy?"

Josh dragged at the pipe, then grinned. "Doing better than expected. Boy's tough. Already sitting up in bed, hanging on to that old .22 rifle. Martha and Amy are spoiling the kid something fierce." He knocked the ashes from the pipe against a hitching post. "You look like a man with a thirst, Travis. I've got a jug hidden from Martha. We can parley over a shot of Kentucky's best."

The two strode down the dusty street, Luther shortening his strides to keep pace with the thump of the marshal's cane. A few minutes later, Luther sat before Josh's battered desk and sipped at the whiskey from the hidden stash.

"How's it look out there, Travis?"

Luther lowered the glass. "Not good. Scarborough's probably still got ten or so men left, all tough hombres. I don't have to tell you how bad we're outnumbered."

The marshal frowned. "We lost another couple of guns in the last day and a half. Neil Braden's showing yellow on us. George doesn't think Braden will fight. How much time you reckon we have?"

"Probably another full day. They could surprise me and get here tomorrow, but I think they'll be laid up and licking some hurts until day after." Luther waved away the marshal's offer of a refill and leaned over to study the sketch they had made earlier of the town's planned defenses. Luther's brows knitted in thought as he studied the map. "Marshal, we've got as good a plan as possible, considering what we have in the way of troops. We'll have Scarborough's bunch in a cross fire. But we need an edge—something to put a little more bite in our trap. I think that edge may be right under our noses. Does that old cannon beside the church still work?"

Josh Turlock's brow furrowed. "We touched her off last Fourth of July. Just powder and wad, though. We don't have any ball or canister."

"Who's your gunner?"

"Carl Alesworth, the lay preacher. Spent some time in the artillery before he got called to spread the Gospel." The marshal shrugged. "Won't do us much good, though. Can't just run down to the fort magazine and pick up a load of powder and shell."

Luther grinned. "We've got a magazine, Marshal. Everything we need is in Holloway's store. He tried to give us over to the enemy. Seems only fair he'd want to make amends and donate what we need. And he won't be needing it anymore. Horseshoe nails, chains, and loose buckshot should make a passable load for an artillery piece."

The marshal's hand doubled around the shot glass in his fist. A glimmer of excitement danced in the deep hazel eyes. "By God, I should have thought of that." He pushed his chair back. "Let's go raid a storehouse. Then I'm calling another town meeting." He chuckled softly. "With a little luck we just might be able to bloody that bunch of outlaws."

Tyler Scarborough sat hunched on his bedroll, a nearly empty bottle at his feet. The whiskey didn't seem to be easing the pain.

When the shooting started, Tyler thought he was a dead man. The big slug had gone clean through Doc Halston and torn a half-dollar-sized chunk from Tyler's upper arm. And when somebody finally rolled what was left of Doc off, Tyler panicked. His head and chest were covered with blood and bits of flesh; it took a few seconds before he realized it wasn't his. The slug had exploded Doc's heart and lungs and spattered the gore over Tyler. Another few inches and the bullet would have taken Tyler square in the chest. He was spooked, hurting, and still smarting from the scare, but he was alive. And he was getting mad clear to the bone.

At least, he reminded himself, he was better off than Doc and the two sentries. And Pete and Curly, who had been brought in facedown over a couple of jaded horses, bushwhacked like a couple of rank amateurs in the rocky canyon gorge north of camp.

Several hours had passed before Tyler realized how bad his bunch had been cut up. He had six dead men and two wounded. One rider had a bullet crease on a hip, another a busted collarbone from when the buffalo rifle slug went through the saddle he tried to hide behind. The two could still ride and shoot, but they'd be hurting bad.

Tyler had pulled into the Horse Springs camp with sixteen men. He had ten left who could still fight. Pain and cheap whiskey boiled the rage in his gut. By God, somebody's going to pay for this, he vowed silently. Nobody does this to Tyler Scarborough and lives to brag on it.

"Moondog's comin' back, boss," Carlos Vasquez called softly.

"About damn time," Tyler groused. "Tell that crazy Apache to get his butt over here."

Minutes later Moondog squatted before Tyler, his black eyes showing no expression. Other members of the band gathered around, faces grim and angry beneath the dirt, traces of burned black powder, and sweat. "Lost the trail five miles out," the Apache said. "That's one tricky man. Tracks just quit, like he'd gone straight up."

"You say *one man*?" Tyler snorted in disbelief. "No way one man could do what was done to us last night."

Moondog shrugged. "This one could. It was the big man. The one who killed your brother."

Tyler spat in disgust. "Hell, Moondog, I thought you were a tracker. Had to be at least two men out there. I heard a buffalo gun and a smaller bore rifle. There had to be at least two shooting at us."

"Same man. Two guns." Moondog fished into a pocket and held a spent cartridge aloft. "One forty-four forty. Other sounded like a Sharps." Moondog shook his head in admiration. "Much man, that one. Carved one of our boys up with a big knife. Broke another one's neck with his bare hands. Maybe we don't want to catch this one. I think he's bad medicine. Could be he's the Moon Wolf."

Tyler glared hard into the Apache's eyes. "Damn your superstitious soul to hell, Moondog," he growled, "you turnin' yellow on me?"

A flicker of anger danced in the black eyes. "Apaches don't quit. Apaches also don't like to get killed." Moondog rose in one smooth motion and strode away.

"Well, boss," Vasquez said, "maybe Moondog's right. Might be best to forget this Cimarron town. There's other places—"

"No, by God!" Tyler's voice almost cracked in his rage. "We're going to take that damn town! And I'm personally going to skin that big son of a bitch alive!"

Vasquez's heavy shoulders lifted in a shrug. "I'm game. Reckon we ought to lay over another day, rest up the men and horses? Nearly rode ourselves and our mounts down trying to catch that jasper. We've got a couple boys feelin' mighty hurtful." The Mexican gestured at Tyler's wounded shoulder. "Day's rest might help that arm of yours, too."

Tyler sighed and reached for the bottle at his feet. "Yeah, I guess you're right, Carlos. Besides, I sent word to La Cueva telling that damn sorry excuse of a sheriff to get his butt over here. Bates is due tomorrow. About time he started earning his money." He sipped at the liquor and struggled to control his impatience. This was no time to get stupid. Not with that big son of a bitch Travis out there somewhere. Not when it was still possible to take him alive. With him out of the way, Cimarron would turn belly-up and whimper. Cut off the snake's head and the rest don't count for much, he thought.

Tyler glanced up at the one-eyed Mexican. "Carlos, I don't want to spend another night in this place. Too much high ground around. You stay. Bring Bates to me at that dry wash five miles this side of Cimarron. The one with the old sheepherder's shack and the rock fence. Know it?"

Vasquez nodded. "I'll find it. What if Bates don't show?"

Tyler's lips clamped in a thin line. "Then you go find the bastard and kill him." Scarborough lifted the bottle, took a hefty swallow, and fought back the flare of nausea it triggered in his gut. He stared hard toward the east, as if he could see through the hills to the community on the river. "Carlos, I'm going to settle accounts with that Travis if it's the last thing I do." He drained the last of the liquor from the bottle and grimaced. "And when I'm through with him, we'll turn that damn town of his upside down."

Tyler squinted up at the burly Mexican. "Carlos, when we ride into Cimarron, you keep an eye on that damn Apache. I want to make sure he doesn't cut and run when we tree his Moon Wolf."

Luther McCall sat on a wooden pew at one side of the small church, his gaze drifting over the small gathering of townspeople inside.

It wasn't much of a fighting force, but it was all he and Josh Turlock had. George Winfield, a strong man but untested by the gun. The two cowboys Luther knew only by first names—Ace and Toby—whose abilities with weapons were also unknown, but who had the look of men who knew how to use guns. Carl Alesworth, the gangly lay preacher. Luther wasn't sure about Alesworth. He knew the man was sincere about his religion. When it came time to take a human life, could he violate one of the commandments he preached? That was another unknown. Luther didn't like unknowns when it was his own hide on the line.

Luther didn't worry about Denver Smith, the wiry cantina owner. The look in Smith's eyes said he'd be ready when the shooting started, and Luther had a feeling the old former cowboy had more than a nodding acquaintance with Colonel Colt and Major Winchester. A man didn't live that long in these parts without knowing how to handle himself.

The look in the eyes of Neil Braden, the café owner, was different. Braden, Luther noted, was flat-out scared to death. He wasn't going to fight. It showed in the nervous darting of the gaze, the constant bob of Adam's apple, and the face the color of flour gravy.

None of the other men of the town had shown up, nor had any of the scattered homesteaders who scratched a lean living from the tough land outside of Cimarron.

Martha Turlock, her eyes flashing, sat beside an outwardly serene Amy Caldwell. Six men and two women to hold off a gang of dangerous hard cases who lived by the gun and fed off violence and death the way other men lapped up biscuits and syrup. All we've got going for us is the element of surprise, Luther thought. He let his gaze drift back to the aging marshal's face as Turlock stood beside the pulpit.

"No, by God," a voice from a pew called. "I'm not gettin' myself killed over some drifter gunnin' a man down. I done told you that, and I ain't heard nothin' here today to make me change my mind. Deal me out, Turlock." Neil Braden rose to his feet, a sweat-stained trainman's cap in hand. "I figure if I leave them alone, they'll let me be."

Josh Turlock's heavy eyebrows bunched in a cold stare. "It won't work that way, Braden," he said. "They'll shoot you down like a dog in the street, along with the rest of us, if we don't stop them."

"I got money. I'll buy my way out." Braden twisted the cap in nervous hands. Sweat shone on his balding head despite the comparative cool of the church interior.

The marshal snorted in disdain. "Braden, I've stomped centipedes with more backbone than you. All right, get out of here. Run off somewhere and hide." The old man's voice took on a cold, formidable tone. The expression in the deep hazel eyes was hard. "But you better hide good, Braden, because you're through in this town. Nobody I know wants to eat with a coward."

Luther started to his feet, his fists doubled, disgust burning in his gut. Neil Braden was about to get the thumping of his cowardly life.

"Let it go, Travis," Turlock said. "You can't force a man to fight."

Luther struggled to control his temper. He knew the marshal was right. You couldn't make a man pick up a gun if he didn't have the guts for it. He sighed and settled back down on the hard pew. Braden shot a quick glance at Luther and shuffled hurriedly from the church.

Josh Turlock glowered at Braden's back as the door closed behind the café owner. Then he sighed. "All right, folks, at least we know where we all stand. Let's get a few details ironed out and be ready when those outlaws come."

Carl Alesworth stood. "Marshal, I already know my job. If you ladies and gentlemen will excuse me, I'll see if I can't talk some sense into Brother Braden's head. Perhaps he is in need of a bit of guidance, so to speak." Alesworth nodded to the women and strode for the door.

Josh stroked his silver handlebar mustache. "Martha, I don't want you and Amy involved in this fight—"

Martha Turlock lurched to her feet. She shook a finger at the marshal. "Listen to me, you old badger," she snapped, "this is my town just as much as it is yours. I got a sick boy to protect. That gang of thugs will kill Jimmy—and probably the rest of us, too—if they take our town. By all that's holy, I'll drop a hammer on the first one who rides within thirty yards of that child! You've got no right to stand up there like God Almighty and tell me to go home and tend my knitting!"

Josh raised a hand to stem the torrent of angry words. "Calm down, Martha. Listen to reason. I just don't want you women to get hurt, that's all."

"You think we won't get hurt whether we fight or not, Josh Turlock? I'm getting my Irish up, you old coot! You just hand me a shotgun and get out of my way!"

Luther had to smother a quick grin. Martha Turlock, he mused, just might be the toughest one of the bunch.

"I'm with Martha, Marshal Turlock," Amy said, her voice soft but firm. "We have nothing to lose. I abhor violence. But if it's the only language those awful men speak, then I believe it is our duty to converse with them on their own level."

Josh Turlock lifted his palms, as if in supplication. He glanced at Luther, saw no encouragement in the pale blue eyes, and shrugged. "Very well, ladies. I know when I'm cornered. We'll find something for you to do. Now, let's go over our plan one more time. . . ."

An hour later, Josh Turlock and Luther McCall stood outside the whitewashed church building and stared down Cimarron's main street. The first lookout had already climbed into the church bell tower, ready to sound the alarm at the approach of any horsemen. Neither man spoke for several moments. Finally, Turlock broke the silence.

"Travis, we could have a bloodbath here," he said softly. The worry was thick in the marshal's tone.

Luther knew Turlock feared failure more than the possibility of getting himself killed. Responsibility for a town and the other lives that made up that town was a heavy load for a man to carry. It was one reason Luther had stayed out of other people's business—until Cimarron started to get under his skin. "Probably," Luther said. "The trick is to make sure the right blood gets spilled. We're as ready as we're going to get."

The weathered marshal reached into a shirt pocket and produced a dented, worn badge. "Been saving this for someone man enough to wear it, Travis. In case anything happens to me, the town's going to need a lawman. Deputy marshal may not be much of a title, but it's enough to get the job done." He held out the tarnished metal star.

Luther shook his head. "I'm not much on the idea of wearing a badge, Marshal. Tends to put limits on what a man can and can't do. Give the damn thing to somebody else." Luther reached for his tobacco sack and started to roll a smoke.

"Sure you won't think it over? Serving as a lawman to help out a town in need might have its advantages to a man in your position, Travis." Turlock raised a knowing eyebrow. "I could put in a good word for you here and there. Might help."

Luther cut a sharp glance at the marshal. "A man in my position, as you put it, has no more use for a badge than a jackass has for a hammer," he said. He scratched a match on the rust-pitted barrel of the old cannon and lit the smoke.

Turlock started to continue the argument, then abruptly paused and nodded down the street. "Well, I'll be damned."

Luther dragged on the cigarette and stared at the two men approaching. Carl Alesworth had a hand clamped under Neil Braden's arm. The café owner's steps were unsteady, his toes dragging. As they neared, Luther saw the swollen left eye, the red swath of a heavy bruise along a cheekbone, the slight trickle of blood from Braden's mouth. The café owner's eyes were glassy and unfocused. Luther glanced at Alesworth's right hand. The preacher's knuckles were skinned.

"Looks like old Neil there ran into a door or something," Turlock said with a quizzical brow raised.

"Something of the sort," the lanky preacher said calmly. "Mr. Braden and I had a bit of a discussion a few minutes ago. He has, I believe, seen the light of his previous folly. I wouldn't count on him to assist, but I do believe now he will be no threat to our crusade."

"Threat?" Luther had a problem keeping the amusement from his tone. He raised his opinion of the preacher a notch. From the looks of the biscuit pusher's face, Alesworth had done what Luther had wanted to do.

Alesworth nodded. "It came to me as a message from the Almighty that Mr. Braden is privy to our plans here. It wouldn't do to have that information fall into the wrong hands, or perhaps a shouted word of warning, no matter how misguided."

"So you massaged his head until he saw the light?"

"I suppose you could say Mr. Braden has been dutifully anointed, Mr. Travis." Alesworth nodded to the marshal. "If I might borrow the key to our small jail cell, Marshal?"

"Sure, Reverend," Turlock said. "It's in the padlock. Don't know if the lock's rusted shut or not. Haven't used it in a spell. What do you plan to do?"

"I thought Mr. Braden might be more comfortable, and out of harm's way, as the guest of our municipality until this unpleasant affair ends."

"You can't just throw a man in jail without reason, Reverend," Turlock said. "What's the charge?"

Alesworth's eyes went wide in mock surprise. "Why, attempted assault, sir. Can you imagine a man actually attempting to strike a man of the cloth with his fists?"

Turlock grinned. "Fair enough."

The two men stood beside the cannon as the preacher led the café owner toward the marshal's office. After a moment,

Turlock chuckled aloud. "I'd never have thought Carl had it in him," he said.

Luther let his own grin show. "Marshal," he said with a nod toward the preacher, "I think you just found your deputy."

CHAPTER
ELEVEN

The hours seemed endless to Luther McCall.

Almost a full day had passed since the first lookout climbed the rickety ladder to the church bell tower, and still the town waited.

Luther stood against the side wall of the church and stared down the street, a brief pause in his constant walking tours of Cimarron. From time to time he had climbed the narrow game trail on the bluff north of town, watching for a dust cloud or some sort of movement on the horizon.

Only the emptiness of the land looked back.

Cimarron was outwardly a ghost town. Those who had dealt themselves out of the showdown with Scarborough's band had fled, or pointedly stayed behind closed and bolted doors. There were no wagons, no horsemen to be seen. The townspeople who had vowed to fight kept near their assigned posts, weapons at hand, and waited. The early afternoon sun hammered hard against the dusty and deserted main street.

Josh Turlock was right, Luther thought as he swiped a soggy bandanna across his forehead. This waiting's worse on the nerves than a full-blown fight would be. The heat of the sun beat down on his shoulders and baked the receiver of the Winchester in his hand until it was almost too hot to hold.

Ripples of heat waves danced over the stone walls of the community water well and shimmered toward the western horizon. A dust devil whipped its miniature tornado's tail past the blacksmith shop and whirled past the porch of Amy Caldwell's boardinghouse. Even the dogs were quiet today. Luther wondered if they could sense the expectation of danger, or if the heat had just worn them down.

He knew the waiting would be worse for many of the others. At least he could keep himself occupied checking on the defenders and moving from place to place to keep watch on areas not visible from the lookout's post in the bell tower.

Everything was in readiness. Josh Turlock waited in the small marshal's office, his .44 Remington loaded and capped. George Winfield sat on a milking stool behind the heavy metal forge and anvil of his smith's shop. Carl Alesworth now stood his turn at the tower vigil. Denver Smith waited at the lone window of his dingy cantina with a scarred Springfield single-shot rifle and a brace of new Winchesters borrowed from the late Otis Holloway's general store. The young cowboy named Ace lay behind the false front facade of Holloway's Emporium, his friend Toby across the street on the roof of the abandoned carriage and harness shop. The entire length of Cimarron's main street was bracketed by guns. Anyone in the street would be under fire from all sides when Luther or Josh Turlock gave the word.

Martha Turlock sat behind the dining table in her home, a wicked-looking, sawed-off, twelve-gauge double shotgun sharing space with her coffee cup. Down the street, Amy would also be waiting, her own twin-barreled smoothbore resting alongside the book opened before her. She was reading Dante again. A good pick, considering all hell could break loose around here any minute, Luther mused. He and Josh had the devil's own time getting the women to move away from the doors and windows and agreeing to cut loose with the smoothbores only if the outlaws broke free of the ambush on the street and tried to take cover.

Even Jimmy Macko was ready to fight. The boy was able to sit up now; he waited beside the window of his room, the little .22 Remington rolling block in his hands. Luther had made him promise to stay in the chair when the fighting started. Jimmy's window opened onto an alley beside the Turlock home. His job was to make sure no outlaw climbed into the house through the window. Luther gave him the assignment because he figured it would keep

Jimmy reasonably safe. The puny little .22 wasn't going to be all that much help to anyone, but it gave Jimmy something to do, to make him feel that he was contributing just like the grown-ups.

Luther was satisfied that the trap was ready to be sprung. He could think of nothing else that needed his attention. He could only hope that the defenders would stick to the plan and not open fire until he or Josh gave the signal. He stiffened at Carl Alesworth's call from the bell tower:

"Rider coming."

Luther stepped from the wall of the church into the street and peered through the heat waves. The horse and rider were like mirages through the shimmer. Something about the man looked familiar, but from this distance Luther couldn't be sure who the horseman was.

Hinges creaked at the door of the marshal's office. Moments later Josh Turlock limped up beside Luther, squinted toward the approaching horseman, and snorted in disgust.

"It's that pissant of a sheriff from over in La Cueva," Turlock growled, the contempt thick in his voice. "Wonder what that damn fool's doing here."

Luther recognized the rider then. Ned Bates fidgeted in the saddle, his head swiveling back and forth as he rode along the deserted street. Bates's hand was on the butt of the Colt on his hip. That's a nervous man there, Luther thought as the horseman drew closer, and nervous men are the most dangerous kind.

Bates pulled his sweaty sorrel to a stop fifteen feet away. "Marshal," he said by way of greeting. His gaze flitted from Luther to Turlock and back again.

"Sort of off your home range, aren't you, Bates?" There was an open challenge in Josh Turlock's tone. "Kind of hot to be making social calls."

Bates swallowed. "Not social, Marshal. Business." He glanced back toward Luther. "I've got a warrant for this man's arrest."

"That a fact? What's he wanted for?"

"Suspicion of murder. He shot Dolph Scarborough."

Turlock turned his head and spat. "Hell, that's no crime,"

the marshal said. "Besides, that paper of yours ain't worth mule piss in Cimarron. Only warrants good here are federal papers. In case you didn't notice, Bates, this is still a territory. And it ain't New Mexico."

Bates flushed. Luther couldn't tell if it was from anger or a flash of fear.

"I got to take him back, Marshal," Bates said. "And the boy, too—Jimmy Macko."

Turlock stared hard into Bates's eyes for several heart-beats. "Who'd Jimmy kill?"

"He's a witness. I got to take him into protective custody."

Turlock reached for his pipe and clamped it between his teeth. "I don't think so. I believe I'll just keep both of them around, Bates."

"Now see here," Bates sputtered, "I'm trying to do you a favor, Turlock. Trying to save your town for you. Give those two up and Tyler Scarborough won't come after the man who killed his brother."

"So Tyler sent you, eh?" Turlock pulled a tobacco sack from his pocket and began to fill his pipe. "I heard you and Tyler had a sort of working arrangement. You run-ning errands for him, too? Along with pushing his stolen stock?"

"Damn you, Turlock! You can't say that!"

The marshal tamped his pipe with a forefinger. "I just did, Bates." He struck a match, puffed the pipe to life, and squinted through the smoke at Bates. "Sheriff, I may be just an old, crippled-up town marshal, but I sure as hell got no use for a man who sells his badge to the likes of the Scarborough gang." He shook out the match and dropped it. "And right now, it looks to me like you got a big problem."

Alarm flashed in Bates's eyes. His face paled. "What are you talking about, Turlock?"

"I'm just wondering how you're going to ride out of here alive."

The last bit of color drained from Ned Bates's face. The corner of his mouth twitched. Luther pulled the hammer of his Winchester to full cock. The metallic clicks were loud in the sudden silence. Bates glanced at Luther; his gaze locked on the muzzle of the rifle. It was trained squarely on his chest.

"Now, see here, Turlock," Bates stammered, "you got no right—"

"Don't need one," the marshal interrupted. "Now, you got your hand on that Colt. You got two choices, Bates. You can pull it and get yourself dead. Or you can ease it out gentle and slow and drop it. I'd break it to you gentler, but I'm tired of jawing. It's too damn hot out here. You're under arrest, Sheriff Bates."

"What—you can't—you got no authority—"

"Pull it or drop it."

Bates's Adam's apple bobbed twice. Then he eased the Colt from his holster and let it drop into the dusty street.

"Get down," Turlock said.

Bates dismounted. The color flooded back into his face as the marshal patted him down, found no hide-out gun or knife, then waved Bates toward the jail cell. "Tyler'll kill you for this, Turlock," Bates blustered as he marched toward the jail.

"Maybe. Maybe not. I don't think Tyler Scarborough's going to waste a lot of sweat over your hide, Bates." Turlock stabbed a key in the padlock on the jail cell. "Brought you some company, Neil," he said to the figure seated despondently on the single bunk. He shoved Bates inside, locked the door, and led the way outside.

"For what it's worth, Marshal," Luther said as the office door closed behind them, "I'm obliged. You could have turned me over to him. It's my fault Scarborough's coming. I'm the one who shot his brother."

Turlock dragged on the pipe. It had gone out. He reached for another match. "Travis, I don't give a tinker's damn what you may or may not have done. I don't think for a minute Scarborough would just ride off if I'd handed you and Jimmy over to that two-bit imitation lawman. I got an idea Scarborough sent his pet pup in here to spy out the lay of the land and see what he might be up against. I like our chances better with Bates in jail."

Luther waited until Turlock struck the match and fired

the pipe again, then cocked an eyebrow at the old marshal. "You've got guts, Josh Turlock. While you were fiddling with that pipe, Ned Bates could have drawn his Colt and put a slug in you."

Josh Turlock puffed out a smoke ring, then glanced at Luther. There was a distinct twinkle in the deep hazel eyes. "Never worried about it much, Travis," he said. "I figured you'd blow a hole in him big enough to ride a jackass through if he tried it. Was I right?"

Luther flashed a wry smile. "Yes. But if I were you, Marshal Turlock, I'd be a little more choosy about the character of the men I put in control of my life."

Turlock chuckled. "To hell with it," he said. "Let's get ready. I got a feeling we're going to be up to our elbows in Scarborough men before long."

Tyler Scarborough squatted in the thin shade of a mesquite tree and scowled up at the big Mexican on horseback. Tyler's shoulder still hurt like sin. Sweat kept trickling into the raw flesh and made it sting something fierce. The whiskey was gone, and now the men were running short of water and grub.

Tyler Scarborough was not pleased.

"So they got Bates in the lockup? Just marched him off like a chicken thief?"

Carlos Vasquez nodded. "That's about the way it happened, boss."

Tyler licked at his cracked lips and finally worked up enough moisture to spit. "Damn that tin star Bates, anyway. At least he could have made a try. No guts." He squinted at the one-eyed Mexican. "How many guns they got down there?"

Vasquez shrugged. "Didn't see anybody but the old marshal and the big man. Nobody else in sight. Looks like the whole town pulled out. What's your pleasure now, boss? Want to put a couple rifles on the bluffs above town and wait for a chance to pick those two off?"

Tyler came to his feet slowly, favoring the sting in his shoulder. "No time for that, Carlos," he said. "We're out of whiskey and running short on water and grub now. There's plenty of that down in Cimarron. And the way I've got it figured, that gold shipment'll be moving out of Trail City in four or five days. We got to be there before then." He toed the stirrup, mounted, and winced at the fresh stab of pain from the damaged shoulder muscles. "You sure you didn't see anybody else down there?"

"Nope. Town's dead as a doornail."

Tyler let a grin crease his chapped lips. "Then we got no problem. I told you boys those candy-assed townspeople wouldn't put up a fight. All we got to do is ride in and take over." He reined his horse about to face the Apache, who waited silently at the edge of the group. "Moondog, take the point. If you don't get bushwhacked on the way, hold up a hundred yards out of town until the rest of us catch up."

Moondog stared into Tyler's eyes for a couple of heartbeats, then kneed his horse into a slow trot toward Cimarron.

Tyler Scarborough waited until Moondog was out of earshot, then turned again to Vasquez. "Carlos, you ride with me. Keep an eye on that damn Indian. He's still spooked from those damn medicine visions. If he tries to run, kill him." He reined his horse around to face the rest of the outlaw group. "Boys, I don't care how many of you throw down on that crippled-up old marshal, but that big son of a bitch Travis is mine. I want to blow his guts out personally. Let's go. It's time to take us over a town."

A hundred yards ahead, Moondog shifted uneasily in the saddle. His hand fell to the haft of the skinning knife on his belt, his gaze flicking from side to side. A sudden flicker of movement in the mesquite jarred him bolt upright; he caught a brief glimpse of gray before the coyote vanished. An icy track raced down his spine. The animal was more than just a coyote. The Moon Wolf hunts in daylight, he thought. Bad medicine. He turned to glance at the outlaw band following. The men rode relaxed, slumped in the saddle. None of them had seen the Moon Wolf. There will be blood today, he thought. Much blood.

Moondog made up his mind. Let the white man sneer. No one could fight a spirit. When the blood time came, Moondog would fight—until there was a chance to run. The Moon Wolf will not drag these bones to its lair tonight, he vowed.

Carl Alesworth spotted the dust cloud a full ten minutes before the horsemen came into view, their shapes distorted by the heat waves. They didn't seem to be in much of a hurry. He couldn't tell from this distance how many men were in the band. It could be as many as a dozen. That meant it had to be the Scarborough gang.

He reached for the blacksmith's hammer at his feet, hefted the instrument, and tapped twice on the brittle metal of the old church bell, holding the edge of the bell in his free hand. The muted clangs rippled over the deserted main street of Cimarron.

The lay preacher didn't wait to make sure the others had heard the signal. He knew they would. He clambered down the rickety ladder to the church floor beneath and hurried through the back door. A few minutes later he stood beside the rust-pitted cannon, a cigar glowing between his teeth. He had never cared much for tobacco. It tasted bitter.

Josh Turlock stepped from the marshal's office and nodded silently to Alesworth. The preacher started as a shape seemed to materialize at his side. He didn't understand how a man as big as the one called Travis could just appear like that from nowhere, unseen and unheard.

"They're coming," Alesworth said softly.

Luther squinted toward the approaching horsemen. He loosened the Colt in its holster and strode toward the well. So the dance is about to start, he thought. I just hope these wallflowers we've got planted around don't get too quick on the trigger. Surprise is the only edge we've got.

He stopped at Josh Turlock's side. The old man had pinned his tarnished star to the outside of his leather vest. He held the ancient Remington percussion pistol at his thigh as he stared toward the riders.

Neither man spoke. Luther moved to one side of the stone well, the marshal to the other. The well was the only substantial cover in the street, a place to duck behind when the shooting started. Only a damn fool or a man soon to be dead stood out in the open when there was a hidey-hole nearby and lead about to fly.

Luther checked the action of the Winchester a final time and saw that a cartridge was chambered and ready. He cocked the weapon and propped it against the back side of the well. This would most likely be handgun work, at least at the start. He glanced over his shoulder. Carl Alesworth stood with his back straight beside the ancient cannon, looking out of place with the fat cigar in his teeth and wearing the absurd swallow-tailed coat and a top hat under the blazing sun. Alesworth nodded almost imperceptibly.

Luther glanced along the sides of the street. He spotted the top of a hat and the thin barrel of a rifle atop the general store and caught the brief "ready" signal from the roof of the abandoned building across the way. The two cowboys were in position. One by one, other signs flashed briefly along the street.

Cimarron was ready. The old marshal who leaned against his cane at Luther's right might never have risen past the rank of private in the war, but he sure as hell could define and staff a defensive position, Luther thought. He slipped the Colt from its holster. The deep crosshatches carved in the grip kept the weapon firm in his hand despite the sweat from his palms.

"Well, Marshal Turlock," Luther said, his tone calm and quiet, "company's here. Think they'll charge us?"

Josh Turlock casually spat. "Maybe, maybe not. I reckon we'll find out soon enough."

The two men fell silent as the horsemen drew near the far edge of town. A few more yards and they would be under the guns of the hidden marksmen. The riders didn't stop; they rode straight toward the two men waiting by the well. Tyler Scarborough was out front, the Apache at his left and the big Mexican at his right. The others fanned out behind in a semicircle.

Fifteen yards from the well Tyler Scarborough pulled his horse to a stop, the .41 Lightning in hand. He sat for a moment and glared in pure hate at Luther. "Step aside,

Marshal, and you won't get hurt," Scarborough said. "It's that big son of a bitch I want."

Josh Turlock racked back the hammer of the big Remington. "Don't think I believe you, Scarborough," he said. Luther heard no fear in the old man's voice. "I reckon you're just going to have to take us both."

Tyler Scarborough barked a curse and lifted his pistol.

Luther swept his own handgun up and squeezed the trigger. The Colt bucked in his hand; Tyler Scarborough grunted aloud as the heavy slug ripped into his chest. At Luther's side the marshal's Remington barked, and a rider tumbled from his horse. Luther thumbed the hammer and slapped a shot at the big Mexican; the man's horse shied and the slug missed.

Then all hell broke loose in Cimarron.

A ragged volley of hurried, wild shots mingled with the curses and yelps of the Scarborough band. A slug plucked at Luther's sleeve as he steadied his aim and drove lead into a tall rider who had Turlock in his sights. The man's body jerked as he yanked the trigger. Luther heard a whack and a grunt at his side and chanced a quick glance at Turlock. The old man had gone down on his side, but the Remington cracked again. Chips of stone flew from the edges of the well, and slugs hummed past Luther's shoulder and ear. Luther crouched, crabbed across the few feet to the marshal, grabbed the old man's belt, and yanked him behind the cover of the well. Now, Carl! Luther shouted silently. He glanced over his shoulder toward the lay preacher.

Carl Alesworth calmly dragged at the cigar, ignoring the lead that kicked dust around him and pinged off the barrel and wheel hubs of the old cannon. He lowered the glowing end of the cigar to the touch hole of the ancient field piece.

The cannon thundered, belched powder smoke, and bounced on its heavy carriage. Luther ducked instinctively as the assorted missiles from the cannon whirred close overhead. Screams of men and injured horses mixed with the crackle of gunfire and the heavy echoes of the cannon blast.

Luther chanced a quick glance around the side of the well. Three horses were down, kicking and squealing. Two more

Scarborough men were in the street, blood pouring from their bodies. A third dismounted rider scrambled clear of flailing hooves and dove for the pistol he had dropped. The big Mexican with one eye drove spurs to his spooked horse, got the mount under control, and charged past Luther toward the lay preacher. Luther shot him in the back, thumbed the hammer, and fired again. The big man fell across the saddle horn, then slid to the ground.

At the corner of his vision Luther saw the Apache whirl his horse and race toward the narrow alley beside the marshal's house. A rifle cracked from a rooftop, and the horse went down. The Apache kicked free, landed on his feet, stumbled as Turlock's Remington barked again, then disappeared from sight. Another man staggered on faltering legs after the Apache. Turlock fired again. The man went down. The remaining Scarborough riders battled to control lunging and bucking mounts, firing wildly as they struggled with the panicked animals.

Three men broke clear and raced toward the far end of town. Luther snapped a shot, missed, and saw the billow of gun smoke from the cantina. Denver Smith's old Springfield emptied one saddle; another man tumbled over the rump of his horse at two quick shots from the blacksmith shop. A Winchester cracked from a rooftop, and the third rider's horse went down. The man scrambled to his feet and sprinted toward the boardinghouse.

Luther dropped his empty Colt into its holster and swept up his rifle. The Winchester thumped against his shoulder; Luther felt the sinking sensation in his gut when the slug missed its mark. The running man was at the steps of the boardinghouse now, slugs from rifles and handguns kicking dust at his heels or thudding into the walls of the home. The man reached the door, flung it open—and tumbled backward as if struck by a heavy fist. A split second later Luther heard the heavy cough of a big-bore shotgun and grunted in relief. Should have picked another house, fella, he thought. He racked a fresh cartridge into the chamber of the Winchester.

A hush fell over the street, broken only by the fading echoes of gunshots, the moans of wounded men and squeals of injured horses. Dense clouds of gun smoke and dust eddied on the breeze, then wisped away. The carnage on the street was a shock even to Luther. Four men lay dead in the dust. One had been cleanly decapitated by a length of whirling chain. His head lay beside a dead horse, the sightless eyes seeming to stare straight at Luther. Another man stirred and moaned, then came to his knees and stared in disbelief at his chest. A dozen small holes seeped blood from the front of his shirt. The horseshoe nails from the cannon blast had riddled him like buckshot. The man whimpered once, then pitched forward on his face, his boots kicking at the dust.

"Marshal," Luther yelled, "are you hit?"

The immediate reply was the bellow of the old Remington almost in Luther's ear. Luther whirled and slapped the rifle stock to his shoulder. The big Mexican stood in the street, legs spread wide, blood smeared across his chest. He held a pistol in his right hand, the muzzle wavering as the man tried to aim at Luther. Tough son of a bitch, Luther thought as he aimed and squeezed the trigger. The rifle slug caught the Mexican just to the left of his one good eye, snapped his head back, and left a spray of red mist in the air for a moment. The big man sprawled on his back.

Josh Turlock's free hand grabbed for a grip on the rough walls of Cimarron's water well. The old man heaved himself to his feet. "No, dammit," he growled, "I'm not hit. Bastards just shot my cane out from under me." Turlock held the smoking Remington in his free hand and glanced around. "Anybody get hit?"

"Nobody but the bad guys," Luther said.

Over the marshal's shoulder Luther saw a shadow move in the alley beside the Turlock house. "Watch it!" he yelled as he reached out and yanked the old man from his feet. He heard the spiteful pop of a small bore weapon a split second before fire flashed from a handgun in the alley. The pistol slug hit the edge of the well, ricocheted, and dug a furrow across Luther's left forearm. Luther swung the rifle and fired almost over the top of the marshal's head. The solid whop of lead against flesh came almost atop the whip crack of the Winchester's muzzle blast. A man staggered from the alley, took two steps, and fell.

"I hit him, Travis!" Luther heard Jimmy's thin yell over the ringing in his ears and the sharp, rolling echo of his rifle shot.

"Good work, Jimmy!" Luther yelled back. "Stay down! Stay away from the window now!"

"What the hell—"

Luther knelt and helped Josh Turlock back to his feet. "Jimmy just pulled your fat out of the fire, Marshal," he said. "That man had you dead in his sights. He would have nailed you before I could get a shot off."

Josh Turlock glanced toward the alley. "Always figured that boy'd come in handy someday," he said.

Luther thumbed fresh cartridges into the Winchester as he stepped cautiously from behind the stone wall. He ran the count mentally: Four down here. The Mexican behind him made five. Two men dropped while trying to run, six and seven; the one Amy had shotgunned, eight; and the man by the marshal's house, nine. Ten men had ridden in. *The Apache,* Luther thought. *He's still out there somewhere.*

One by one, the other male defenders of Cimarron made their way cautiously into the street. Luther hoped Amy wouldn't come out. The scene was too gory for a woman like her to see. Five minutes later he had finished his quick tour of the battlefield. Two of Scarborough's men were left alive, one wounded, the other still stunned by the fall when his horse went down. Josh Turlock, using an outlaw's rifle as a makeshift cane, led the way as George Winfield and Denver Smith dragged the two injured men toward the Cimarron lockup. Going to be mighty crowded in there tonight, Luther thought with satisfaction. The only injuries to the defenders were the shallow bullet gouge on Luther's left forearm and a nick from a near miss above the ear of the cowboy called Toby. Toby was grinning, the trickle of blood from the nick unnoticed. Those two cowboys will have something to tell their grandkids about now, Luther thought.

Luther strode quickly to Amy Caldwell's boardinghouse, called out at the door, and then stepped inside. Amy stood behind the table, the shotgun still in her hand, her eyes wide. The muzzle of the shotgun trembled.

"It's all right now, Amy," Luther said.

She looked at him, tears brimming in the blue eyes flecked with gold. "Travis, I killed that man out there."

"You had no choice, Amy. He would have killed you."

She lowered the shotgun, placed it on the table, and came into his arms. She buried her face in his shoulder. Luther felt the spastic twitches of her body as she sobbed. "My God—such a terrible thing."

There was nothing Luther could say. He just held her until she regained her composure and finally pulled away to arm's length. "I'm sorry, Travis—I didn't plan to be so weak." She reached up to wipe away a tear and suddenly blanched. There was a smear of blood on her hand. "Travis, you're hurt!"

Luther glanced at the shallow gash on his arm. "It's nothing. Don't worry about it."

"No, I'll get some water—"

"There's no time for that, Amy," Luther interrupted. "There's still one of Scarborough's men out there. The most dangerous one of the bunch. I've got to go after him."

"But why, Travis? Surely he wouldn't dare come back, after—after this."

"It's a chance we can't take." Luther's tone went cold and hard. "He was one of them, Amy. This war isn't finished yet."

CHAPTER TWELVE

The Apache knelt at the lip of a shallow arroyo overlooking the scum-covered pond of a stale seep in the creekbed below, chest heaving as he tried to gasp air back into abused lungs.

He had always felt pride in his endurance of foot, his ability to alternately trot, run, and walk for hours without stopping. It was an ability few still possessed in these times of the horse, a heritage drawn from centuries of his tribal ancestors. But today there was a difference.

He was fleeing the Moon Wolf.

Moondog ignored the raging thirst that dried his tongue and cracked his lips until his breathing slowly returned to normal. His black eyes shifted from side to side as he studied his back trail.

He saw nothing, but took no comfort in the fact. The Moon Wolf was out there. He could feel its presence. He had seen the Moon Wolf in the town called Cimarron. The Moon Wolf stared at him through pale blue eyes, not the fiery, flashing coals of his dreams. The blue eyes were cold. They looked through a man, saw deep into his soul, and cast a chill upon the blood.

Moondog shook his head, trying to banish the memory of that cold blue stare from his mind. He tried to tell himself it was not the Moon Wolf he had seen, only a man. But his mind wasn't listening.

Pain pounded through the wound in his side with every beat of his heart. The pistol slug had struck low, just above the hipbone, and torn through the muscles. Moondog knew there would be a blood trail. He had run two miles before he dared pause long enough to scoop up a handful of sage and mesquite leaves, stuff them into the bloody hole, and wrap them in place with his shirt. Blood still seeped from the wound, but it no longer flowed.

Moondog scrubbed a hand across his eyes, trying to sharpen his vision. He stood for another few minutes, staring back along the convoluted trail he had laid for the past two hours. It would be hard for a man to follow, he knew. It would not be so difficult for the Moon Wolf.

Finally, the Apache turned and strode to the greenish waters of the seep below. He knelt, pushed the pond scum aside, and plunged his lips and chin into the lukewarm, stinking water. It tasted sweet on his parched tongue. After a few swallows he pulled back. In a few more minutes he would drink all he could hold. He did not know when he would find water again.

Moondog knew he was in serious trouble if the big man with the blue eyes came. Moondog had only one weapon, the knife on his belt. He had lost his rifle and pistol in the ambush in the town. He was afoot and without food in a land he did not know, where water and game were scarce. Overhead a pair of buzzards circled, riding the wind currents. There was no other sign of life. He stooped and drank again. When he could hold no more, he stood and studied the land. The shallow arroyo twisted its way north, winding toward what his elders called the big grass country beyond the horizon.

Moondog set off at a brisk walk along the arroyo. Somewhere ahead, there must be a place of refuge. Or a place to fight. The Apache knew he could not run forever. The Moon Wolf could.

Luther McCall leaned in the saddle to study the faint moccasin tracks beneath the clump of mesquite. The tracks were fresher now.

The trail had been easy to follow in the first couple of hours of the hunt. The blood trail had been clear. The droplets lay dark on sun-baked grass and sand. The Apache had made no attempt to hide his tracks; it seemed that he was running blindly, like a man in terror. That wasn't like an Apache, Luther thought. The idea bothered him a bit, a nagging worry that wriggled deeper into his gut.

Luther had tracked animals before, as well as men. There was no difference. A wounded man, like a wounded animal, would eventually stand and fight. And a wounded animal was dangerous game.

He kneed Chili into motion. The brown had broken into a sweat, the hair on its neck and shoulders black from moisture. Luther wasn't worried about the horse's stamina, but he would need to find water soon. Chili could go several days without feed when necessary, but no horse could go beyond its need for water. All Luther had was the canteen tied to his saddle. His own lips had begun to crack from the grinding sun, but he made no attempt to reach for the canteen. The water was for Chili in case there was none to be had on the trail ahead.

An hour later, Luther pulled Chili to a stop and mouthed a soft curse. The trail had doubled back toward Cimarron, then vanished. This Apache's good, Luther thought with grudging admiration. Let's find out just how good he really is. He kneed Chili into a slow walk, riding an ever-widening circle. Another half hour dragged past. Luther almost missed the sign despite his constant search. A single droplet of blood rested on the tip of a mesquite leaf. Luther dismounted and touched a fingertip to the drop. It was fresh, little more than an hour old. He was gaining ground on the Apache.

Luther slipped the hold-down thong from the hammer of his Colt and stood for a moment, staring into the distance. He saw nothing, but it was as if he could feel the Apache's presence. The Indian wasn't close. The sense of nearness was not that strong. But he had been here, not long ago. It was enough. Luther knew he had found the door to the Apache's mind. It was as if he suddenly were walking in the man's moccasins, knew where he would go next.

Luther swung back into the saddle. "All right, you slick son of a bitch," he whispered aloud to the unseen Apache, "I've got you figured now."

Moondog crouched beside a clump of Spanish dagger at the lip of the arroyo and stared in disbelief and growing fear at the figure in the distance.

The white man had found the track.

The Apache squirmed from beneath the sharp spines of the dagger clump and stood. A hundred yards away the arroyo twisted suddenly to the east and dipped; at the sharpest and deepest part of the bend a dense clump of mesquite clung to the edge of the rocky soil. The wind was from the south, blowing from the big man's back. The brown horse would not pick up the smell of man. Moondog knew the time had come. There was no place left to run. There he would kill the evil spirit that haunted his dreams—or be devoured by it.

Moondog ran toward the bend of the arroyo, ignoring the pain that lanced through his side with each step. The pain was of no consequence now. He was about to face the Moon Wolf.

The thought brought a silent shiver to Moondog. He scrambled up the eight-foot bank at the bend of the arroyo and settled in to wait. He slipped the knife from his belt and tested the edge with a thumb. The keen edge brought the first sense of confidence Moondog had felt since the hunt began. It is no spirit, he told himself grimly, it is only a man. Still, Moondog was uncomfortable.

He had no time to sing his death song.

The man on the horse drew nearer. He rode at a slow walk now, his gaze alternately raised to sweep the countryside nearby or dropped to study the tracks on the arroyo floor. His rifle was still in the saddle boot, his pistol still holstered.

Moondog shifted the knife to his left hand and wiped the sweat from his palm against his pants leg. The white man was close; only a few more feet. Moondog crouched deeper, his muscles tensed to spring.

The white man was alongside the mesquite clump now. Moondog gripped the knife and hurled himself at the big body a few feet below.

The brown horse shied at the last instant; Moondog's blade missed the man's neck. The Apache's body slammed into the big man. The impact knocked him from the horse and sent both men sprawling on the sand. The white man's half-drawn pistol spun away as their bodies landed with a jar. Moondog whipped the knife blade toward the man's chest, felt the heavy jolt as a forearm slammed into his knife hand and knocked the thrust aside. A fist seemed to come from nowhere. Lights flickered before Moondog's eyes as hard knuckles crumpled the cartilage in the bridge of his nose. He staggered under the impact; the white man's thick forearm rammed against Moondog's neck and shoved.

The powerful heave sent Moondog sprawling as if he were only a child. The Apache rolled and came to his feet as the big man rose, catlike. The white man's right hand shot to his belt. Sunlight flashed against the huge blade in the man's hand. Moondog felt a sudden sense of power. No man could match him in a knife fight. At such times the thin steel blade in his hand took on a life of its own.

The two men circled little more than arm's length apart, each with his eyes locked on the other's face. Neither spoke. The silence of the arroyo was broken only by the scuff of boot and moccasin against sand and the steady, controlled breathing of the two men.

Moondog lunged, his knife aimed at the belly of the big man; the white man twisted to his left, blocked the thrust with his left forearm, and whipped the big blade toward Moondog's chest. Moondog jumped back. He felt the icy track of the blade tip across his chest. The big man was quick, as fast as any man Moondog had ever faced.

The two men again shuffled in small circles, both cautious. Moondog felt a growing respect for the white man, thought he saw the expression mirrored in the pale blue eyes that stalked his every move. Moondog sensed an opening in the man's defense and whipped his blade forward; steel clanged against steel as the white man parried the swing. Moondog reversed the direction of his knife and grunted in satisfaction as the blade sliced through the big man's shirt just above the belt. The white man sprang back. A red stain spread across his side where Moondog's blade had bit.

Moondog felt the surge of confidence in his chest as he stalked the big man. It would be a simple thing now. The white man had felt the sting of steel. Soon Moondog would be on his way, the brown horse between his knees and a good rifle and pistol riding with him.

Moondog feinted a slash from the side. The big man dropped his blade a few inches to parry the cut. Moondog whipped the knife from its original course, rammed the blade straight toward the white man's chest—and hit nothing. The big man spun a complete circle and whipped his own blade upward. The shock of the steel against bone jarred Moondog back on his heels. He stood for an instant and stared, uncomprehending, at the blade that had spun from his hand. Then he felt the first burn of pain; his heart skidded as he glanced at his wrist. Blood pumped in bright spurts from severed arteries. The hand dangled, useless, its tendons slashed through.

Moondog raised his gaze. Light flashed on steel and the ice tracked again, this time across his throat. Moondog saw the gush of blood. He could not breathe. He sank to his knees. Moondog saw the cold glitter of pale blue eyes that suddenly turned amber, and then red, and shot small embers of fire toward his chest. He stared as the white man's face changed; the Moon Wolf's fangs reached for his throat, foam slavering the gaping jaws. The world went red, then black.

Luther McCall stood above the Apache's body for a moment, breathing hard from the exertion of the fight. Then he casually bent and wiped the blood from his blade against the Indian's leg. He retrieved his handgun, puffed the dust from the action, then sheathed the knife and pulled up his shirt. The cut on his side was shallow and clean, the skin barely broken. He ignored the fire building in the cut and in the bruises on his hips and shoulders. He looked around.

Chili stood fifteen yards away, nostrils flaring at the scent of blood, bridle reins trailing. The brown's front hooves pranced nervously as Luther approached, but the horse made no effort to bolt and run.

Luther reached out and patted the horse's neck before gathering in the reins. He lifted the canteen and took a small swallow. "Well, Chili," he said, "the war's over. We can go home now."

Luther McCall mounted and reined Chili toward Cimarron. He realized with a start that it was the first time he had used the word "home" out loud in years. . . .

The big man and the boy sat beneath the shade of a sprawling cottonwood on the bank of the Cimarron River and listened to the chirr of cicadas in the nearby trees.

The heat wave had broken several days ago, and now the breeze from downriver was refreshingly cool. Luther McCall couldn't remember the last time he had been content to just sit and do nothing.

Well, that wasn't quite right, he figured. Fishing with a boy was doing something. It just wasn't a thing that required the expenditure of much physical or mental effort.

Luther leaned back against the trunk of the tree and tugged his hat down lower over his eyes. "Better keep an eye on that float, Jimmy," he said. "Looks like you're getting a bite."

Jimmy Macko snapped to attention like a good cow horse trotting toward a herd. He stared at the sliver of dry wood that served as a cork as if he could will the fish to take the hook below.

The boy was healing fast. The bullet wound was still puckered and pink-edged, but it seldom hurt him anymore. He had regained that constant energy that young boys never seemed to run short of, Luther mused. Hardly a day had passed in the last week that the two hadn't been hunting, riding just for the hell of it and to enjoy the feel of a good horse under saddle, or shooting. Jimmy Macko was a natural with a rifle. There wasn't a pack rat or cottontail in miles safe from that little Remington of his.

The bob suddenly dipped out of sight.

Jimmy yanked hard on the cottonwood limb fishing pole. The stiff limb bent sharply.

Luther sat bolt upright. "Easy, Jimmy," he called, "looks like you've got the granddaddy of them all on the line. Don't yank the hook out; just let him work against the pole."

Jimmy's brow furrowed in intense concentration as he

battled the unseen fish. The line made sharp hissing sounds as it tore first one way and then the other through the reddish waters of the fishing hole. Luther figured the fish would win.

He was wrong.

Ten minutes later Jimmy had wrestled his latest catch onto the bank. It was a big catfish, better than twelve pounds. It lay on its side, the oversized mouth opening and closing, barbels twitching. It was, Luther thought, one ugly sucker.

He reached out and squeezed the boy's upper arm. "That's some fish, son," he said. "We can eat on this one for a week." Luther wasn't crazy about catfish, but Amy and Martha cooked it in a way that made it palatable. He and Jimmy already had four on the makeshift stringer that dangled from an exposed tree root. Two of them were channel cat, smaller but better fighters—and a bit tastier—than the big flathead now gasping on the bank. Luther had always wondered about that. Were the fish gasping for air, or for water? He gave up the question. Only the fish knew.

Jimmy lifted the fish's head and pried the hook from its mouth. Handling a catfish wasn't for the weak of heart, Luther knew. They had spines on the fins that could draw blood. They were slick and slimy and slightly disgusting to the touch. And while they didn't have teeth like a pike or gar, they could still make a boy's fingers smart if they caught them between those rough jaws.

Jimmy grunted as he hefted the fish. Its tail flopped against the stained knee of his pants. The boy had a wide, pleased smile on his face as he held the catfish out for Luther's inspection. "He's a good'un," the boy said.

"One of the best I've ever seen. And mind your English, or Amy'll fuss at you again."

A grimace flickered across the boy's face. "Yes, sir. Seems like a woman'd have better things to do besides fuss over how a body talks."

Luther chuckled. "That's their job, Jimmy. If it weren't for women there wouldn't be much civilization in the world, and there sure wouldn't be any manners. Want to call it a day and go skin some catfish?"

Jimmy shook his head. "They're bitin' too good today. I'd like to get one more nice one. They won't go to waste. I promised the preacher and Denver Smith we'd bring them some." He hauled the stringer partway out of the water and threaded the slender rope through the fish's gills and out through the mouth, then lowered the stringer back into the deep, still water beside the tree. Jimmy baited his hook with a fresh chunk of raw liver from the rabbit he had shot earlier and tossed the line into the water.

Luther leaned back against the tree, content, and pulled his tobacco sack from his pocket. The bullet scrape on his forearm and the shallow cut from the Apache's knife had healed clean in the three weeks since the big fight in Cimarron. Luther rolled his smoke, lit it, and sighed. He knew he was getting too comfortable in this town; he had even put on a few ounces of fat around his middle at Amy's table. Her bed wasn't the worst place in the world to spend the night, either. Luther hadn't slept in his own room in two weeks. He hadn't planned it that way, but he had a lingering suspicion that Amy had. Come to think of it, he mused, she had been looking healthier and happier over the last couple of weeks. Something seemed to be agreeing with her. And she *did* snore, even though she denied it right and left. He only brought it up in private, of course.

Amy now knew who he really was—the whole story. But she still called him Travis, even in private. Luther wasn't sure whether that was force of habit or because she didn't want to accept the truth. Women had some strange ways about them sometimes. But Amy wasn't pushy about anything, which was more than he could say about most women he had known. She accepted him for what he was, scars, warts, and all. She hadn't mentioned anything permanent, or even hinted at it. Luther didn't know whether to be upset or pleased about that. She hadn't even badgered him to go to Sunday church services, even though she never missed one herself.

They'd been discreet about the new sleeping arrangement and careful not to show more than casual friendship when they were out in public. If people in Cimarron suspected anything was going on between them, they were smart enough not to say it in Luther's presence. He was getting too damn protective of Amy Caldwell, he scolded himself.

Cimarron itself seemed happier and more relaxed of late. Ace and Toby, the two cowboys, had found themselves a new line of work. The former Holloway's Emporium and General Store was now the Corral Supply Company. Neither of them knew a lot about keeping books and stocking shelves, but Denver Smith was teaching them. Their prices were fair and their goods first-rate. And they had found a stout hickory cane with an ornately carved stag handle which they promptly presented to Josh Turlock to replace the one shot to splinters by Scarborough's bunch. Luther had a feeling those two cowboys would never work a roundup again.

Ned Bates was back in La Cueva, escorted to the state line by Marshal Josh Turlock and invited never to return to Cimarron. Luther figured the sheriff would accept the invitation. Josh held the whip hand on Bates in several ways—not the least of which was the Remington .44 on the old man's hip.

Neil Braden hadn't survived the coward brand. Two days after Josh Turlock let him out of jail, Braden sold the café to a young couple new to town and rode out without looking back. The place was a sight cleaner now, and the quality of the food hadn't dropped much. The new cook was as talented in the kitchen as she was pretty to look at. The café was usually crowded these days. The two old-timers who had disappeared before the fight—"the trouble" as it was now known in Cimarron—were back at their spit-and-whittle bench, peering with curious suspicion at those who strode past their station.

Come to think of it, Luther realized, Cimarron was getting more crowded by the day. It was actually growing. Three new families with several kids among them had moved into town. Two other couples with kids had settled on homesteads less than an hour's ride out. There were new faces on the street every day, it seemed, and enough youngsters to justify opening a school in the church. Martha and Amy had volunteered to serve as teachers. Jimmy had been the first youngster to sign up. The kid soaked up knowledge and books like most boys his age collected dirt and skinned knees.

Denver Smith's business didn't seem to have dropped off much, either. The cantina was still dingy, still dark, and still pleasantly quiet. Josh Turlock didn't let professional gamblers hang around Cimarron. One cardsharp had stepped off the weekly stage and mail coach a few days back. Josh had stepped the gambler back on it in a hurry. The cantina poker games were still friendly, small-stakes affairs. Luther had sat in a couple of times just to while away a long afternoon. He figured he was maybe a dollar ahead, which told him the games were honest. He hadn't done any serious card playing in those sessions.

Josh Turlock sat in on a few hands. The old man was a better than fair poker player, which caught Luther a little off guard. He casually wondered how many different trails Josh Turlock had ridden before he settled down in Cimarron.

There was no doubt in Luther's mind that Turlock knew Luther's story, probably as well or better than Amy did. But the marshal kept it to himself. Turlock still wasn't overly friendly to Luther, but he wasn't antagonistic, either. With the Scarborough gang finished and Cimarron peaceful again, the two had lapsed back into their former relationship. It was based on mutual respect. Josh Turlock knew Luther wasn't a man to mess with. Luther had the same opinion of the old gimpy marshal. White hair, leathery face, bum leg and all, Josh Turlock was a hell of a man.

Luther waited patiently as Jimmy landed two more fish. The first one to take his hook was a little popcorn cat, barely eight inches long. Jimmy made him promise to grow a little bit, then tossed him back. He kept the second one, then coiled his fishing line.

"That's enough," Jimmy said. He sighed. "Now's the hard part. Cleaning 'em."

Luther grinned at the tousle-haired youngster. "Man has to pay for his fun one way or the other, Jimmy." He rose and dusted the dirt and bits of leaves from his pants as Jimmy grunted to haul the heavy-laden stringer onto the bank. "I'll give you a hand, son. I caught my share, so I guess I've got half the work."

Luther hefted the stringer in his left hand. It was heavier than he had expected.

"Let's go show Martha before we clean 'em, Travis," Jimmy said, a pleased and excited glow in the wide-set brown eyes.

"Sure thing. I expect Martha will be right proud of you." He dropped his free hand onto the boy's shoulder. "Not many women have a provider as good as you."

The boy didn't reply, but Luther felt Jimmy's back stiffen with pride as they strode toward town. They stepped to the side of the road as the weekly stage rumbled past on its way to its next stop in New Mexico. The driver waved a friendly greeting. Luther returned the salute.

Martha did an adequate amount of "oohing" and "aahing" over the day's catch before chasing Luther and Jimmy out back to clean the fish. Luther washed up as Jimmy set out to deliver the whitish-pink carcasses to his friends, then said good night to Martha and stepped into the street. The sun was still a couple of hours above the horizon. He had time for a cool beer before supper. It would be a good way to put the cork in a fine day, he figured.

He nodded cordially to a couple of people as he made his way toward the cantina. Down the street, the door of the boardinghouse opened. Amy stepped onto the porch carrying a tablecloth and waved a greeting. Luther waved back. Amy shook out the tablecloth and spread it on the porch railing to catch the last hours of sun.

Luther was at the door of the cantina when the call came from behind him: "Hey, McCall!"

Luther stiffened. He turned to his left, slipping the hold-down thong from the Colt's hammer with a thumb as he moved. A man stood across the street. He was slightly built, with a smear of stubble on his young face. The .45 Peacemaker in his right hand was big and new.

"Are you talking to me, mister?" Luther's tone was casual, almost conversational.

"Damn right I am, McCall."

"I'm afraid you've mistaken me for someone else, friend," Luther said. "I don't know the name."

"The hell you don't. I know you. It's my job to know people like you."

Luther's eyes narrowed. He raised himself onto the balls of his feet. Doesn't have the look of a lawman, Luther thought. Bounty hunter, most likely. He stared at the gunman, measuring the man. Drawing against a man who already had a pistol in hand was bucking a cold deck. Whoever this jasper was, he had the upper hand. For now. Rage simmered in Luther's gut. The man had no right to mess up such a good day.

"Mister, you've got the wrong man." Luther's tone went cold and hard. "I don't want any trouble."

"Then step out from in front of that door, slow and easy, and there won't be any." The wiry man gestured to the side with the hand that held the gun. The quick glimpse was all Luther needed. The damn fool hadn't bothered to cock the Peacemaker.

Luther took a step to his right and made his move. The Colt whispered from his holster and bucked against his palm. The wiry man staggered back a step as Luther's .45 slug hammered into his gut. The man regained his balance, his thumb fumbling at the hammer of his pistol. Luther didn't fight the recoil. He thumbed the hammer back, let the muzzle drop, and squeezed the trigger. His second shot knocked a puff of dust from the gunman's shirt pocket and hurled him back against a wall. The man's thumb slipped from the hammer. The Peacemaker blasted harmlessly into the dust of the street. Luther took his time—half a heart-beat—lined the sights, and shot the man a third time. The gunman slid down the wall, the pistol dropping from his fingers. He twitched a couple of times and lay still.

Luther approached the downed man with caution. He had seen men take a slug through the heart and still manage to fire several shots and run twenty yards before going down.

The caution wasn't needed. The gunman was dead.

Luther glanced up the street toward the boardinghouse. Amy leaned against the rail, a hand raised to her mouth.

Luther heard footsteps behind him. He spun, then lowered his weapon as Denver Smith stepped into the street, the old Springfield rifle in his hands. Smith strode past Luther and stared down at the dead man.

Moments later, Luther heard the familiar thump of Josh Turlock's cane in the street. Turlock had the old Remington in his hand, the hammer drawn to full cock.

"What happened here?"

Denver Smith glanced up from the dead man. "Jasper here threw down on Travis," he said, his voice matter-of-fact. "Had him cold, it looked to me. Luther didn't even have his gun in his hand. Drew and nailed him three times. Damn me if that ain't some shootin'. You could lay a quarter on those last two bullet holes."

Josh Turlock stared for a moment at Luther, his gaze icy. "That the way it happened, Travis?"

Luther flipped open the loading port of his Colt, worked the ejector rod, and kicked the three empty cartridges into the dust. He nodded. "That's the way it happened, Marshal." He thumbed fresh loads into the Colt and dropped it back in his holster.

Turlock looked like he was about to speak, then leaned over and stared at the dead man. "You know him, Travis?"

Luther shook his head. "Never saw him before."

Turlock knelt stiffly at the dead man's side and went through his pockets. Luther watched as the marshal laid out a few coins, a folding knife, and a pocket watch. Turlock glanced at a bloodstained paper from the gunman's right shirt pocket, then silently stuffed the paper into his own vest. After a moment the marshal heaved himself to his feet. "No identification," he said. Turlock lowered the hammer of the Remington and holstered the weapon. "Denver, get a couple of the boys to drag this man out of the street. Travis, come with me." He turned and limped toward the marshal's office and jail.

Luther went along.

Turlock sat behind the desk and stared at Luther in silence for a moment. Then he plucked the paper from his vest pocket and tossed it onto the desk. "That fellow knew who he was after, Travis," the marshal said. "Bounty hunter out to pick up a few dollars."

Luther unfolded the yellowed, blood-stained paper and studied it for a moment. It was like others he had seen. He dropped the wanted notice back on the desk. "He wasn't very good at his job," Luther said.

Josh Turlock snorted in disgust. "Young guns. Dumb as a rock. I reckon that's how come they don't get to be old men. No great loss." He slid a creaky desk drawer open, reached inside, and brought out another wanted flier. He studied it for a moment in silence, then looked up. "Pretty detailed description, Travis. I think they missed the weight by about twenty pounds."

Luther shrugged. "That was a long time ago, Marshal. So what do we do now?"

Turlock picked up both papers, turned, and opened the door of the old wood stove behind the desk. He tore both sheets in several pieces, tossed them into the stove, and reached for a match. "We made a deal, Travis. I keep my word." He fired the match and flipped it into the stove. The scraps of paper flared.

Turlock reached back into the desk, brought out a thick envelope, and tossed it to Luther. "This came on the mail coach today. It's yours. Reward money on the Scarborough bunch. Eight hundred and twenty dollars." The marshal leaned back in his chair and stared at Luther. "That'll take a man a long way from Cimarron," he said.

Luther stared back. The marshal didn't blink. "Are you telling me to leave town, Marshal?" Luther asked.

"We had a deal. So far, we've both kept our ends of the bargain. Let's just say I'm asking you if there's some part of the country you haven't seen yet."

Luther fought back the burning aggravation in his gut. The marshal was right; they had cut a deal. Still, it rankled a bit to be run out of town like a common thief. Luther sighed. "It's a big country. I suppose there's a chunk of it I haven't seen." He tucked the envelope containing the reward money into his shirt pocket.

"You going to count that?"

Luther half smiled. "I don't think you'd cheat a man, Josh Turlock. I'll take your word for it." He turned for the door, then paused and looked back. "I'd like to say good-bye to Jimmy and Amy."

Josh Turlock shrugged. "Take your time. Sunup tomorrow will be soon enough. And, Travis—if you happen to see this Luther McCall fellow, tell him I think maybe he got a raw deal on those wanted posters. Seems to me those guys he killed needed it. But ask him not to come back to Cimarron. We don't need trouble here."

"I'll do that, Marshal. If I run across him somewhere. I doubt he'll be coming through these parts, though." Luther touched fingertips to hat brim in salute and strode through the door.

Amy Caldwell stood at Luther's stirrup, her hand on his knee. Tears pooled in her gold-flecked blue eyes. "Travis, are you sure—you can't stay? For a little while longer, at least?"

Luther swallowed against the tightness in his throat. It had been hard enough to say good-bye to Jimmy. Hard enough to put a lump behind his Adam's apple. And the lump wasn't getting any smaller.

"I'm sure, Amy," he said. "It wouldn't work out. There will always be others like that bounty hunter. Or young men looking to make a gunfighter reputation by putting me down. You deserve more from life than that."

Luther patted the back of Amy's hand for the last time, then picked up the slack in the reins. "Keep an eye on Jimmy for me, will you?"

Amy nodded. A tear trickled down her cheek. "Take care of yourself out there, Travis."

Luther nodded and reined Chili about. The brown humped his back, but didn't pitch. Luther's new packhorse, a leggy sorrel he'd bought from George Winfield, fell into step at Chili's right hip.

At the top of the hill in the river breaks a half mile west of Cimarron, Luther pulled Chili to a stop and twisted in the saddle to stare back.

Cimarron had the look of a nice, quiet little frontier town.

Luther McCall sat erect in the saddle for a long minute,

looking back. Then he sighed. "Some things are just not meant to be, Chili," he said softly. "So where do we go from here?"

Chili snorted and bobbed his head. "Okay," Luther said, "northwest sounds fine. Should be some fine elk hunting up in the Tetons this year."

Luther touched heels to the brown.

This time he didn't look back.

FROM THE AWARD-WINNING AUTHOR OF
RIVERS WEST: THE COLORADO, HERE IS THE SPRAWLING
EPIC STORY OF ONE FAMILY'S BRAVE STRUGGLE
FOR THE AMERICAN DREAM.

THE HORSEMEN

Gary McCarthy

The Ballous were the finest horsemen in the South, a
Tennessee family famous for the training and breeding of
thoroughbreds. When the Civil War devastated their home
and their lives, they headed West — into the heart of Indian
territory. As a family, they endured. As horsemen, they
triumphed. But as pioneers in a new land, they faced
unimaginable hardship, danger, and ruthless enemies...